"What did ya wanna talk about?" Eli asked.

"Us. I wanted to talk about us."

"There is no *us,* Laura," he said, shaking his head. "I thought you understood I can't leave my faith."

"I do understand, Eli," she said softly. "I'm sorry for asking you to give up your way of life."

Eli's lips curved into a smile. "Someday you'll meet the right man, and—"

Laura covered his mouth with her fingers. "I've already found the right man."

His eyebrows raised in obvious surprise. "You have? That's *gut.* I wish you all the best."

She compressed her lips in frustration. Was Eli deaf, dumb, and blind? Couldn't he see how much she wanted him? She grasped both of his hands and gave them a squeeze. "The man I've found is you, Eli. I want no other, and I never will."

"But, Laura—"

WANDA E. BRUNSTETTER lives in Central Washington with her husband, who is a pastor. She has two grown children and six grandchildren. Her hobbies include doll repairing, sewing, ventriloquism, stamping, reading, and gardening. Wanda and her husband have a puppet ministry, which they often share at other churches, Bible camps, and Bible schools. Wanda invites you to visit her website: http://hometown. aol.com/rlbweb/index.html

HEARTSONG PRESENTS

Plain
and Fancy

Wanda E. Brunstetter

To Lucy Ann—
May the Lord
bless you richly!
Love,
Wanda E. Brunstetter
8-14-02

Heartsong Presents

In loving memory of my good friend, Sharon Hanson, whose love for her "special" child was an inspiration to all.

A note from the author:
I love to hear from my readers! You may correspond with me by writing:

> Wanda E. Brunstetter
> Author Relations
> PO Box 719
> Uhrichsville, OH 44683

ISBN 1-58660-529-1

PLAIN AND FANCY

Cover design by Victoria Lisi and Julius.

PRINTED IN THE U.S.A.

one

Laura Meade opened her laptop, entered the correct password to put her on-line, and began the E-mail she'd been meaning to write for the past week.

> *Dear Shannon,*
>
> *I'm finally settled in at the Lancaster School of Design. I think I'm going to like it here. Not only is the college rated in the top ten, but the valley's beautiful, and the Amish in the area are unbelievable! The Plain women I've seen wear simple, dark-colored dresses, with little white hats on their heads. The men wear cotton shirts, dark pants with suspenders, and either a straw or black felt hat with a wide brim. They drive box-shaped, gray buggies pulled by a horse. They look like something out of the Dark Ages!*
>
> *Tomorrow I'm going to the Farmers' Market. I hear it's a great place to get good buys on handmade Amish quilts. I may even be able to acquire some helpful deco-rating ideas.*
>
> *Hope you're doing well. I'm looking forward to seeing you at Christmas.*
>
> *Your friend,*
> *Laura*

Laura thought about sending an E-mail to her parents, but she'd talked to them on the phone an hour ago. Moving away from the desk, she picked up a brush from the dresser and began her nightly ritual of one hundred strokes through her long, thick tresses.

She glanced around. Even the smallest room at home was bigger than her dorm room, but she'd only be here two years. Then she could go home and redecorate the whole town of Minneapolis if she wanted to.

"It's stifling in here," Laura moaned. She dropped the hairbrush to the bed and opened a window. A slight breeze trickled through the screen, but it did nothing to cool the stuffy room. Here it was the first week of September, and the days were still hot and humid.

Fall had always been Laura's favorite time of the year. In fact, someday she hoped to decorate her own home with harvest colors. The kitchen windows would be outlined with sheer, yellow curtains. The living room, dining room, and bedroom floors would be covered with thick, bronze carpet. She wanted Early American furniture, and there would be plenty of paintings on the walls.

Mom and Dad had allowed her to travel halfway across the country to attend Lancaster School of Design. There were several good schools closer to home, but when Laura heard about this one, so near the heart of Amish land, she wanted to come. She was sure she could learn some unique decorating ideas from the interesting culture of the Plain People.

Laura glanced at the picture of Dean Carlson, sitting in a gold frame on top of her dresser. He was the newest partner at Meade Law Firm, and they'd been dating off and on for the last six months. Dean hadn't been happy about her moving to Pennsylvania, even though it would only be for a few years.

A loud knock jolted Laura out of her musings. With a sigh, she crossed the room and opened the door.

A young woman with short, curly blond hair stood in the hallway. "Hi, I'm Darla Shelby, your next-door neighbor."

Laura shook her hand. "I'm Laura Meade."

"Since tomorrow's Saturday, I thought I'd hop in my sports car and drive to Philly for some serious shopping. Would you like to tag along?" Darla offered.

The mention of a car caused Laura to brood over her own

expensive car, parked in the garage at home. She wished she would have driven it to Pennsylvania, but her parents had insisted on her flying.

"I realize we've only met," Darla continued, "but I figure what better way to get acquainted than in the middle of a Philadelphia shopping spree."

Laura leaned against the doorframe as she contemplated the tempting offer. "I appreciate the invitation, and I'd love to go some other time, but I've got my heart set on seeing the farmers' market at Bird-in-Hand tomorrow. I understand some of the Plain People go there."

Darla nodded. "Those Amish and Mennonites are quite the tourist attraction." She pointed at Laura. "I'll let you off the hook, but I hope you'll take a rain check."

"I promise, but tomorrow, why don't you go to the market with me?"

Darla wrinkled her nose. "No way! I'd rather be caught in the middle of rush-hour traffic on the turnpike than brush elbows with a bunch of farmers!"

Laura wiggled her eyebrows. "Those *farmers* do look pretty interesting."

"Maybe so, but they're not interesting enough for me to waste a whole day on." Darla turned toward her own room, calling over her shoulder, "Whatever you do, Laura Meade, don't let any of that Amish culture rub off on you!"

ॐ

A ray of sun filtered through the window, causing Laura to open her eyes. She peeked at the clock on the bedside table. It was nearly nine o'clock! She'd slept much later than she planned. Jerking the covers aside, she slipped out of bed and headed straight for the shower. Later, as she studied the contents of her closet, Laura had a hard time deciding what to wear. She finally opted for rust-colored slacks and a beige tank top. She accentuated the outfit with a gold necklace. Her long, auburn hair was pulled back on the sides and held in place with tan, pearl-studded combs.

"Nothing fancy, but presentable," she said to her reflection in the mirror. "Amish country, I hope you're ready, because here I come!"

&

When Laura stepped from the cab, she stood in awe of her surroundings. Part of the parking lot was full of Amish buggies. It looked odd to see them lined up, with modern looking cars parked a few aisles away. She wished she'd remembered her camera, for this was a sight to behold!

Heat and humidity were already beginning to weigh the morning down, and she was relieved to step inside the farmers' market and find the building much cooler.

The first table Laura discovered was run by two young Amish women. They were selling an assortment of pies and cookies. Both wore their hair parted down the middle, then pulled back into a tight bun. Small, white caps were perched on top of their heads, and their dresses were long, blue cotton, with black aprons over the top. One of the women smiled and asked if she'd like to sample something.

Laura stared longingly at a piece of apple pie. "They look delicious, but I had breakfast not long ago." The truth was, she was always counting calories. One bite of those scrumptious pastries and she'd probably gain five pounds. She moved on quickly, before temptation got the better of her.

The next few tables were run by non-Amish farmers. Their things didn't interest Laura much, so she found another table, where an elderly Amish woman was selling handmade quilts.

"Those are gorgeous!" Laura exclaimed. "How much do they cost?"

The woman showed her each one, quoting the prices, which ranged from four to nine hundred dollars.

"I'm going to buy one," Laura said without batting an eyelash. "I don't want to carry it around while I shop, though. Can you hold this one for me?" She pointed to a simple pattern, using a combination of geometric shapes, done in a variety of rich autumn colors.

"What's this called?" she asked.

"That's known as 'Grandmother's Choice,' " the Amish woman replied, her hand traveling lightly over the material.

Laura nodded. "I like it—a lot. I'll be back for it before I leave, but I can pay now if you'd like."

The woman smiled. "Pay when ya come back." She placed the quilt inside a box, then slipped it under the table.

It was getting close to lunchtime, so Laura decided to look at one more table, then find something nonfattening to eat.

The next table was loaded with a variety of hand-carved items. Laura glanced around for the person in charge but didn't see anyone. She picked up one of the finely crafted birdhouses and studied the exquisite detailing. When a young Amish man popped up from behind the table, she jumped, nearly dropping the birdhouse. He was holding a box filled with more bird-houses and feeders. A lock of sandy brown hair fell across his forehead, and his deeply set, crystalline blue eyes met Laura's gaze with a look that took her breath away. Her cheeks grew hot, and she quickly placed the birdhouse back on the table. "I–I was just admiring your work."

A hint of a smile tweaked the man's lips, revealing a small dimple in the middle of his chin. "My name's Eli Yoder. I'm a wood-carver and carpenter, and I'm ever so thankful God gives me the ability to use my hands for somethin' worthwhile."

Though she had been to church a few times, Laura was not particularly religious. Nibbling on the inside of her cheek, she merely nodded in response.

"Are ya lookin' for anything special? I also have wooden flowerpots and ornamental things for the lawn." Eli lifted one up for her inspection.

Laura stared at his hand, clutching a windmill whirligig. Her gaze traveled up his muscular arm. Below his rolled-up shirtsleeve, his tanned arms were feathered with light brown hair. She licked her dry lips and forced her wayward thoughts to come to a halt. "I—uh—live in a dorm room at the Lancaster School of Design," she stammered. "So I really don't have a need for birdhouses or whirligigs."

"I don't think I've ever heard of that school."

"I'm learning to be an interior decorator," she explained, drawing her gaze to his appealing face, then back to the items on the table.

When he made no comment, she looked up again and saw that he was staring at her with a questioning look.

"My job will be to help people decorate their homes in attractive styles and colors."

"Ah, I see. Do ya live around here, then?"

She shook her head. "My name's Laura Meade, and I'm from Minneapolis, Minnesota. I've already studied some interior design at one of our local community colleges, and I'm here to complete my training."

There was an awkward silence, as they stared at one another.

"Eli, there you are! I thought we were supposed to meet for lunch," a beseeching woman's voice called out. "I waited outside, but ya never showed. I figured I'd better come a-lookin'."

Eli turned to face a young, blond-haired Amish woman, dressed similar to the other Plain women Laura had seen earlier. "I'm sorry, Pauline," he said. "I got busy talkin' with this customer and forgot about the time." He considered Laura a moment. "Is there anything you're wantin' to buy?"

"I was just looking," she murmured.

"Well, *wass machts aus?*" Pauline said, frowning. "Eli, if you're finished here, can we go have lunch?" She took a few steps closer, brushing her hand lightly against Eli's arm.

Eli nodded. *"Jah,* Pauline." He glanced back at Laura. "It was nice chattin'. I wish ya the best with your studies." He turned away, and the Amish couple ambled off.

Laura tried to still her racing heart as she watched them disappear. *How did it get so warm in here? And how in the world could someone as plain as that Amish man be so adorable?*

❧

As Eli and Pauline exited the building, he glanced over his

shoulder. The young English woman was still standing beside his table. *She's sure a fancy one. Fancy and very pretty. I wonder why someone like her would be so interested in birdhouses?*

"Eli, where do ya wanna eat lunch?"

Pauline's question and slight tug on his shirtsleeve brought Eli's thoughts to an abrupt halt.

"I thought you carried a picnic basket," he said peevishly.

"I did, but I wasn't sure where ya wanted to eat it."

He shrugged. "It makes no difference."

"Let's go to the park across the street. There's picnic tables and trees to shade us from the hot sun."

Eli gave no response, and she grabbed his sleeve again. "What's wrong? You're actin' kinda *naerfich*."

"I'm not nervous," he assured her. "I've just got a lot on my mind."

Pauline slipped her hand through the crook of his arm. "After you've had a few bites of fried chicken, ya won't be thinkin' of nothin' but my good cookin'."

Eli feigned a smile. "Kissin' wears out, but cookin' don't." Truth be told, he really wasn't in the mood to eat just now, but he wouldn't let on to Pauline. He was sure she'd worked hard making the picnic lunch, and he'd promised to eat it with her. Besides, it was a silly matter that had turned his thoughts away from his date. A few drumsticks and a plate of potato salad would sure as anything get him thinking straight again!

☙

The expensive Amish quilt Laura purchased at the market was placed across the bottom of her bed, making it a definite focal point in the tiny dorm room. It reminded her of the young Amish man who'd been selling woodcrafted items. As she sat at her desk trying to study, Laura found herself wishing she'd bought one of his birdhouses.

Her fingers drummed restlessly across the desktop. As ridiculous as it might seem, Laura had been attracted to Eli Yoder. It was stupid, because she and the Amish man were worlds apart. Besides, the young woman he'd been with seemed awfully possessive. *She could even be his wife.*

Laura fought the urge to fantasize further and forced herself to concentrate on the monochromatic swatches of material lying before her. It wouldn't be good to get behind on her studies because of a passing fancy with someone she'd probably never see again.

❧

Laura was kept busy with classes and what seemed like never-ending homework. It had been several weeks since she'd ventured into Amish land, but today was Saturday, and she was determined to have some fun. She was fascinated by the Plain People and decided to check out a few gift shops in a nearby Amish community. This time she made sure she had her camera.

Laura took a taxi to the village of Paradise. The first store she entered was a souvenir shop, filled with excited tourists. It had numerous shelves full of Pennsylvania Dutch trinkets, and a rack of postcards, with photos of Amish and Mennonite farms, Plain People, and horse-drawn buggies. Laura bought several, with the intent of sending them to family and friends back home.

Her next stop was The Country Store, which was set up something like a modern convenience store. It was stocked with gift items, groceries, and plenty of snack food.

Laura wandered toward the back of the store. To her amazement, the shelves were lined with oil lamps, bolts of plain cotton material, women's black bonnets, men's straw hats, boxes of plain handkerchiefs, and several pairs of work boots. One whole section was stocked with barrels full of whole grains, and along one wall were several straw brooms and a variety of gardening tools.

"The Amish must do their shopping here," Laura murmured, feeling suddenly self-conscious, like she didn't belong. She moved quickly toward the door.

Outside on the sidewalk, two Amish girls were playing jump rope. They took turns using the rope, sucking on lollipops while they awaited their turn.

They're so cute. I just have to get their picture. Laura pulled a camera from her purse, focused it on the children, and was about to snap the picture when someone grasped her shoulder.

"We don't approve of havin' our pictures taken."

Laura spun around. A pair of penetrating blue eyes bore down on her. Her heart skipped a beat. It was the same Amish man she'd met at the farmers' market a few weeks ago!

"I remember you," Eli stated. "You were at the market, lookin' at my birdhouses."

Laura offered Eli her best smile. "I'm sorry if I did wrong by trying to photograph those cute little girls."

"The Amish don't believe in havin' their pictures taken," he reaffirmed.

"What about all the pictures on postcards?" She withdrew one from her purse. "Isn't that an Amish man working in the fields?"

Without even glancing at the postcard, Eli shot back, "Photographers have many ways of gettin' the pictures they want. Sometimes they hire non-Amish to dress like us. Some use close-up lenses, so they can take pictures without us even knowin'. Others offer payment. This happens a lot with our *kinder.*"

"Your what?"

"The children."

Laura frowned. "I don't understand. If your religion doesn't approve, why would it be okay for kids to take money?"

"Not all Amish are as strict about the rules. A few believe it's all right for the *kinder* to have their pictures taken. Like many other religions, some of our people make certain worldly concessions." Eli shook his head. "Some even leave the faith in order to live like the English do."

Laura was tempted to ask if that would be such a bad thing, but she didn't want to say anything offensive to the Amish man.

Eli motioned toward a wooden bench near the building.

"Would ya wanna sit awhile? I'll take my birdhouses inside, then we can have a glass of root beer. That is, if you'd like one."

Laura nodded enthusiastically. Of course she'd like a root beer! Especially when it would give her more time to question Eli. She dropped to the bench and leaned forward with her elbows resting on her jean-clad knees. She watched Eli head to the parking lot, where his horse and buggy stood waiting. He made two trips into The Country Store, shouldering large cardboard boxes filled with birdhouses and feeders. When he emerged for the last time, he was carrying huge mugs of foamy root beer. He handed one to Laura and sat down beside her.

"I noticed your buggy is open—sort of like a carriage," she remarked. "Most of the Amish buggies I've seen are closed and kind of box-shaped."

Eli grinned. "That's my courtin' buggy. Pop gave it to me on my sixteenth birthday."

"What's a courting buggy?"

"English boys get a driver's license, and maybe a car when they turn sixteen. We Amish get an open buggy, so's we can start courtin'. You English call it *datin'*," he explained.

"Have you been dating very long?"

"Are you wantin' to know my age?"

Laura felt the heat of embarrassment creep up her neck, but she nodded anyway.

"It's okay. I don't mind ya askin' one bit. I'm twenty-three, and Pop says I oughta be married already." Eli chuckled and lifted the mug of root beer to his lips.

So, he's single, and just a year older than me. Laura wasn't sure why, but that bit of information gave her a great deal of pleasure. "How come you're not married?"

Eli shrugged. "Guess I haven't found anyone who can put up with me."

"I'm sure some young lady already has her eye on you." Laura was thinking of the Amish woman who'd been with Eli at the market. She'd seen the way that Plain gal looked at him.

Eli laughed. "I don't know 'bout that, but I do know I'm not ready to settle down to marriage yet." He smacked his lips and changed the subject. "Umm. . .this is sure *gut* root beer. Thomas Benner, the store owner, makes it himself."

Laura took a sip. *"Gut?* What does that mean?"

"It's the Pennsylvania Dutch word for good," he explained.

She smiled. "It is *gut* root beer, and your buggy's sure nice-looking. How does it ride?"

Eli rewarded her with a warm smile. "Would ya like to find out?"

"I'd love that!" Laura jumped up, then whirled around to face him. "Would it be all right? It's not against your religion or anything?"

Eli's smile widened, causing the dimple in his chin to become more pronounced. "Many Mennonite and Brethren take money from tourists, in exchange for a buggy ride. So, I know of no rule sayin' ya can't take a ride in my buggy." He winked at her. "If someone should see us, they'll probably just think you hired me for a ride."

❧

Eli helped Laura into the left side of the open buggy, then he climbed up on the right and gathered the reins. With a few clucks to the beautiful gray and black gelding, they were off.

A slight breeze caught the ends of Laura's golden bronze hair, whipping them gently around her face. Eli felt his chest constrict. *This English woman is sure appealin'. Why, it's almost sinful to be so beautiful. I'm wonderin' why she would even want to be seen with someone as plain as me.*

Eli felt a twinge of guilt for allowing himself the simple pleasure of admiring her beauty, but he couldn't quit thinking how it might be to know her better.

"This is awesome!" Laura exclaimed. "I never would have dreamed riding in a buggy could be so much fun!"

He glanced over at her and smiled. *"Jah,* I like it, too."

When they'd gone a short distance, Eli turned the buggy down a wide, dirt path, where there were no cars, just a carpet of flaxen corn on either side.

"Where are we going?"

"To Paradise Lake. It's wonderful *gut* this time of year." Eli flashed her another smile. "I think you're gonna love it!"

❧

Laura leaned back in her seat, breathed deeply of the fresh air, and drank in the rich colors of the maple trees dotting the countryside. "I think the warm hues of autumn make it the loveliest time of the year," she murmured.

Eli raised his dark eyebrows. "Such fancy words you're usin'."

She laughed. "Should I have said, it's wonderful *gut?*"

"*Jah,* wonderful *gut!*" Eli pulled the horse to a stop in a grassy meadow near the small lake. "Here we are!"

"You were so right," she gasped. "It *is* beautiful here!"

Eli grinned like a child with a new toy. "In the summer it's a *gut* place for swimmin' and fishin'. We like to skate on the lake when it freezes over in wintertime, too."

Laura drew in another deep breath. "It looks like the perfect place for a picnic."

"My family and I have been here many times." Eli glanced over at Laura. "Would ya like to get out and walk around?"

"That sounds nice, but I rather like riding in your courting buggy," she said with a sigh of contentment. "Can't we just drive around the lake?"

"Sure, we can." Eli got the horse moving again.

As they traveled around the lake, Laura began to ply him with questions about the Amish. A gentle breeze rustled the trees, and she felt her heart stir with a kind of excitement she'd never known. She wasn't sure if it was the fall foliage, the exhilarating buggy ride, or the captivating company of one very cute Amish man that made her feel this way. One thing for sure, she felt a keen sense of disappointment when Eli turned the buggy back to the main road.

"Do you like wearin' men's trousers?" he asked suddenly.

She glanced down at her blue jeans and giggled. "These

aren't men's trousers. They're made for a woman, and they're quite comfortable." When Eli made no comment, she decided it was her turn to ask a question. "What's your family like?"

He grinned. "I have a *gut* family. There's Pop and Mom, and I have an older sister, Martha Rose. She's married to Amon Zook, and they've got a three-year-old son. I also have two younger brothers who help Pop on the farm while I'm workin' at the Strausberg Furniture Shop in Lancaster."

"I'd like to see your farm sometime." The unexpected comment popped out of Laura's mouth before she had time to think about what she was saying.

When Eli's brows drew downward, and he made no response, she wondered if she'd overstepped her bounds. As much as she would like it, she'd probably never get to meet Eli's family or have another opportunity to ride in an Amish buggy.

It seemed like no time at all and they were pulling into The Country Store's parking lot. Eli jumped down and came around to help Laura out of the buggy. When his hands went around her waist, she felt an unexpected shiver tickle her spine. "Thanks for a wonderful *gut* ride. I'll never forget this day."

Laura started across the parking lot and was surprised to see Eli walking beside her. They both stopped when they reached the sidewalk. "I'd better find a telephone booth and call a taxi. I'm supposed to meet a friend for supper in about an hour," she said with a note of regret.

Eli clicked his tongue. "Your friend is some lucky fellow."

She gazed deeply into his eyes. "It's not a man I'm having supper with. It's a girl from school."

He smiled. "I was wonderin'—would ya be interested in goin' back to Paradise Lake next Saturday? We could take a picnic lunch."

Laura could hardly believe her ears. Had he really asked her on a date? Maybe not a date exactly, but at least another chance to see him.

"That would be nice," she said, forcing her voice to remain steady. "What should I bring?"

"Just a hearty appetite and a warm jacket. I'll ask Mom to fix the lunch, because she always makes plenty of food."

"It's a date." Laura blushed. "I mean—I'll look forward to next Saturday. Should we meet here in front of The Country Store, around one o'clock?"

"*Jah,* that'll be fine," he answered with a nod.

"Until next Saturday then." Just before Laura turned toward the phone booth, she looked back and saw him wave. She lifted one hand in response and whispered, "Eli Yoder, where have you been all my life?"

two

Laura's eyelids drooped as she leaned against the headrest in the backseat of the taxi. A picture of Eli's clean-shaven face popped into her mind. His twinkling blue eyes, sandy brown hair, and that cute little chin dimple made him irresistible.

She opened her eyes with a start. What was she thinking? She couldn't allow herself to fantasize about Eli Yoder. He was off limits—forbidden fruit for a modern, English woman. *Then why am I thinking about him? And why did I ever agree to go on a picnic with him next Saturday?*

As hard as she tried, Laura seemed unable to squelch the desire to see Eli one more time. She would learn a bit more about the Amish, they would enjoy a *gut* picnic lunch, soak up the beauty of Paradise Lake, and it would be over. They'd never see each other again. She would only have memories of the brief time she'd spent with an intriguing Amish man. It would be a wonderful story to tell her grandchildren someday. She smiled and tried to visualize herself as a grandmother, but the thought was too far removed. The only thing she could see was the face of Eli Yoder, calling her to learn more about him and his mysterious religion.

❧

The family-style restaurant was crowded, and Laura was late. She stood in the clogged entryway, craning her neck to see around the people in front of her. Was Darla already in the dining room? Sure enough, she spotted her friend sitting at one of the tables.

When Laura arrived, Darla was tapping her fingers against her place mat. "Sorry to be late," Laura apologized. She pulled out a chair and sat down quickly.

"Were you caught in traffic?"

"Nope. I went for a ride in an Amish buggy this afternoon. I guess we lost track of time."

Darla's eyebrows furrowed. "We?"

"I was with Eli Yoder. He's the cute Amish guy I met at the market a few weeks ago. I'm sure I mentioned it."

Before Darla could comment, Laura rushed on. "We had a great time. The fall colors at the lake were gorgeous." She glanced down at her purse and frowned. "I had my camera with me the whole time, but I forgot to take even one picture."

Darla gazed at the ceiling a few seconds, then she looked back at Laura. "You're starstruck, but I hope you realize you're making a big mistake."

"What are you talking about?"

"I can see you're crazy about this Amish guy, and it can only lead to trouble."

"I'm not *crazy* about him!" When Laura noticed several people staring, her voice softened. "I did enjoy his company, and the buggy ride was exciting, but that's all there is to it. I hardly even know the man."

Darla studied her menu. "I hope you're not planning to see him again."

"We're going on a picnic next Saturday, but it's no big deal."

Darla leaned across the table. "Don't do it. Cancel that date."

Laura's mouth dropped open. "It's not a real date. It's just an innocent picnic. Besides, I can't cancel. I don't have his telephone number, so I have no way of getting in touch with him." She grabbed her menu, hoping this little discussion was finally over.

"Most Amish don't have telephones," Darla reminded. "Do you know they live like the pioneers used to? They don't use electricity, no phone, no cars—"

Laura held up her hand. "I get the picture. Can we change the subject now?"

Darla's voice dropped to a whisper. "I want to say one more thing."

Laura merely shrugged. Darla was obviously not going to

let this drop until she'd had her say.

"I've lived in this area all my life, so I know a little something about the Amish."

"Such as?"

"They don't take kindly to outsiders involving themselves in their lives."

"Eli doesn't seem to mind."

Darla gritted her teeth. "His folks sure would mind if they knew he was seeing an English woman. I'll bet they don't though, do they?"

Laura hated to be cross-examined. None of this was Darla's business. "I have no idea what Eli's told them."

"The Amish are private people. They live separate, extremely plain lives. They don't like worldly ways—or worldly women for their men." Darla shook her finger. "You'd be smart to nip this in the bud before it goes any further."

Laura remained silent. She didn't need Darla's unwanted advice, and she knew *exactly* what she was doing.

❧

Laura had been sitting on the wooden bench in front of The Country Store nearly an hour. *Where is he? Maybe he isn't coming. Maybe Darla's right and he's decided it's best not to have anything to do with a "worldly" woman. I'll give him another five minutes, then I'm leaving.*

She scanned the parking lot again. There were several Amish buggies parked there, but they were all the closed-in type. Eli's courting buggy was nowhere in sight. She watched as several Amish families went into the store. *How do those poor women stand wearing long, dark-colored dresses all the time? And their hair—parted straight down the middle, then pulled back into a tight bun. I wonder why they wear those little caps perched on top of their heads? I couldn't stand looking so plain!*

It was 1:50 when Eli's buggy finally pulled into the parking lot. Laura felt such relief, she was no longer angry. She waved and skittered across the parking lot.

Eli climbed down from the buggy. "Sorry to be so late. I had to help with chores at home, and it took longer than expected."

"It's okay. You're here now, that's all that matters."

Eli gave her a boost, then went around and took his seat. He glanced up. "There's not a cloud in the sky, so it should be a *gut* day for a picnic." He beamed at Laura, and her heart skipped a beat. "Did ya bring a jacket? The sun's out, but it's still pretty chilly."

Laura shook her head. "I'm wearing a sweater. I should be fine."

Eli picked up the reins and said something in Pennsylvania Dutch to the horse.

"What'd you say?"

His face turned crimson. "I told him I was takin' a beautiful young woman on a ride to the lake, so he'd better behave himself."

Laura's heart kept time to the *clip-clop* of the horse's hooves. "Thank you for such a nice compliment."

Eli only nodded in response.

They traveled in silence the rest of the way, but Laura found being in Eli's company made words seem almost unnecessary.

Paradise Lake soon came into view. If it were possible, the picturesque scene was even more beautiful than it had been the week before. Maple leaves were dispersed everywhere, like the colorful patchwork quilt lying on Laura's bed. The sun cast a golden tint against the surrounding hills, and a whippoorwill called from somewhere in the trees. Laura relished the sense of tranquility as it washed over her like gentle waves against the sand.

Eli helped her down, and she slid effortlessly into his arms. Raising her eyes to meet his, her breath caught in her throat at the intensity of his gaze. Her pulse quickened, and she grabbed her camera, hoping the action would get her thinking straight again. She photographed the scenery, being careful not to point the camera in Eli's direction. It was a sacrifice not to snap a few pictures of his handsome face. How fun it would be to send one to her friend, Shannon.

Eli pulled a heavy quilt and a huge picnic basket from under the buggy seat. He motioned Laura to sit on the ground, where he'd stretched the comforter. The contents of the basket revealed more food than two people could possibly eat, and Laura knew she'd be counting calories for the rest of the week. As Eli spread a green tablecloth over the quilt, she eyed the meal in anticipation. He set out containers of fried chicken, coleslaw, dill pickles, brown bread, Swiss cheese, baked beans, and chocolate cake. Then he handed Laura a glass of iced tea, some plastic silverware, and a paper plate.

Eli bowed his head in silent prayer, so she waited for him to finish before she spoke. "It was nice of your mother to prepare this. Especially since she doesn't even know me."

Eli reached for a drumstick. "I didn't tell Mom about you."

"Why not?"

He removed his straw hat and placed it on the quilt. "I don't think my folks would like me seein' someone outside the faith."

Laura couldn't hide her disappointment as she bit her bottom lip. "I guess I'll never get to meet them."

"I'd like you to see where I live and meet my family, but takin' you there might cause trouble."

She gave him a sidelong glance. "If you didn't tell your mother about me, then why'd she pack such a big lunch?"

"I told her I was goin' on a picnic, but I'm sure she was thinkin' it was with someone else." Eli reached for another piece of chicken. "Is there anything more you'd like to know about the Amish?"

Laura sighed deeply. Apparently, Eli Yoder wasn't that different from other men. If he didn't like the way the conversation was going, he simply changed the subject. "When did your religion first begin?" she inquired.

"Our church got its start in the late sixteen hundreds, when a young Swiss Mennonite bishop, named Jacob Amman, felt his church was losin' some of its purity," Eli began. "He and several followers formed a new Christian fellowship, later known as 'Amish.' So, ya might say we're right-wing cousins of the Mennonites."

Laura nodded as Eli continued. "The Old Order Amish, which is what my family belongs to, believes in separation of church and state. We also expect Bible-centeredness to be an important part of our faith. A peaceful way of life and abidin' to all nonworldly ways are involved, too."

Laura frowned. "Like no telephones or electricity?"

Eli nodded. "We believe it's the way Christ meant for the church to be. A few Amish businessmen do have a phone," he amended. "They either keep it in the barn or in a small shed outside their home."

Laura ate in silence for a time, savoring the delicious assortment of food and trying to digest all that Eli had shared. She knew about some Protestant religions and had attended Sunday school a few times while growing up. However, the Amish religion was more complex than most. She found it rather fascinating, in a quaint sort of way.

The wind had picked up slightly, and Laura shivered, pulling her sweater tightly around her shoulders.

"You're cold," Eli noted. "Here, take my coat." He removed his jacket and draped it across her shoulders.

Laura fought the impulse to lean her head against his strong chest. The temptation didn't linger long, for the sound of horse's hooves drew her attention to an open buggy pulling into the grassy area near their picnic spot.

A young Amish woman, wearing a dark bonnet and an angry scowl, climbed down from the buggy. Laura thought she recognized the girl, and her fears were confirmed when Eli called, "Pauline, what're you doin' here?"

"I was lookin' for you, Eli Yoder! I stopped by your farm, but Lewis said you'd gone to Paradise Lake for a picnic. I couldn't think who ya might be with, but I see clearly who's taken my place." Pauline planted both hands on her hips and frowned. "I'm mighty disappointed, Eli. I thought this was *our* place. How could ya bring a foreigner here?"

Laura's mind whirled like a blender on full speed. She'd never thought of herself as a foreigner. After all, this was America, and she was an American through and through.

Eli jumped up and moved toward Pauline. He placed one hand on her shoulder, but she brushed it aside. "She's that Englisher you were showin' birdhouses to at the market, ain't it so?"

Eli glanced back at Laura. His face was bright red. "Pauline Hostetler, meet Laura Meade."

Pauline's lips were set in a thin line. She glared at Laura as though she were her worst enemy.

Laura didn't feel much like smiling, but she forced one anyway. "It's nice to meet you, Pauline."

"Ich will mit dir Hehm geh," Pauline said, looking back at Eli.

"I can't go home with you. I came with Laura, and I've gotta take her back to town after we finish our picnic," he explained.

Pauline turned away in a huff. "And to think, I borrowed my brother's buggy for this! I deserve much better." She scrambled into the buggy. "Enjoy your *wunderbaar schee* picnic!"

"Jah, des Kannich du!" Eli called.

Laura sat there, too stunned to speak and trying to analyze what had just happened. Pauline Hostetler was obviously Eli's girlfriend. Laura watched as she drove out of sight, leaving a cloud of dust in her wake.

As Eli dropped to the quilt, Laura offered him a tentative smile. "Guess I owe you an apology."

"For what? You did nothin' wrong."

"I caused a bit of a rift between you and your girlfriend."

Eli shifted on the blanket. "Pauline's not really my girlfriend, though I think she'd like it to be more. We've been friends since we were *kinder.*"

"But you saw how upset she got. She was clearly jealous."

Eli shrugged. "I'm sorry if she's jealous, but I've done nothin' wrong, and neither have you."

"Nothing but have a picnic with a *foreigner*," Laura said sarcastically. "I couldn't understand the words you two were speaking. What were you saying?"

Eli toyed with the end of the tablecloth. "Let's see. . . She said, *'Ich will mit dir Hehm geh*—I want to go home with you.' Then she told us to enjoy our *'wunderbaar schee,'* or 'wonderful nice' picnic. To that, I said, *'Jah, des Kannich du,'* which means, 'Yes, I will.' "

"She spoke some Pennsylvania Dutch to me at the market the other day, too."

"Do you remember the words?"

Laura squinted as she massaged the bridge of her nose. "I think it was something like, *'Wass, machts us.'* She looked kind of irritated when she said it."

"Wass, machts aus," Eli corrected. "It means, 'What does it matter?' "

"Pauline doesn't like me."

He frowned. "How can ya say that? She don't even know you."

Laura groaned. "She knows you, and she's obviously in love with you. I think she's afraid I might be interested, too."

Eli eyed her curiously. "Are ya?"

Laura scooted across the quilt until she was shoulder to shoulder with Eli. "Yes, I am interested. You're different from any man I've ever met." She slid in front of him, so she could gaze into his blue eyes. "I don't want to make trouble for you, so it might be better if we say good-bye and go our separate ways."

Eli reached for her hand. "You're the most beautiful, exciting woman I've ever met. I don't want ya to go walkin' out of my life." He rubbed his thumb slowly across her knuckles, causing little shivers to spiral up her arm.

"Me neither," she said softly.

"Even though it's not possible for us to start courtin', I don't see why we can't keep seein' each other as friends," Eli commented. "It wouldn't really be breakin' any rules."

Laura blinked. She hadn't expected him to offer that much. "How do you know your family won't disapprove? I mean, an Amish man making the acquaintance of a worldly English foreigner?"

Eli shrugged. "I don't know what they'd say for sure, but there's one way to find out."

Laura leaned closer, so her face was mere inches from Eli's. "What's that?"

"We can finish our picnic lunch, then drive over to my place. You can meet my family, before Pauline tells them her version of our picnic."

Laura's stomach clenched, and she willed herself to breathe normally. Was this what she really wanted? What if Eli's family didn't like her? If they made him stop seeing her, even as a casual friend, how would she ever convince him to leave the Amish faith?

Now where did that thought come from? I hardly even know Eli Yoder. Besides, he seems happy with his plain lifestyle. Why would he be willing to give it up for some fancy Englisher like me?

Laura made a conscious effort to concentrate on eating a bit more of the delicious assortment of picnic foods. She would worry about counting calories and changing Eli tomorrow. If she was going into the enemy camp today, it may as well be on a full stomach.

three

The Yoders' farm was situated on sixty acres of dark, fertile land. The fields were planted in alfalfa, corn, and wheat, reminding Laura of a quilt—rich, lush, orderly, and serene. The expansive white house was surrounded by a variety of trees and shrubs, while an abundance of autumn blooms dotted the flower beds. A windmill not far from the home turned slowly in the breeze, casting its shadow over the tall white barn directly behind the house. There were no telephone or power lines on the property, but a waterwheel grated rhythmically in the creek nearby, offering a natural source of power. There was also a huge propane tank sitting beside the house. Laura assumed it was used for heat or to run some of the Amish family's appliances.

"This is it," Eli said with a sweeping gesture. "My home."

Laura's gaze traveled more thoroughly around the orderly looking farm. There were sheep and goats inside a fenced corral, and chickens ran about in a small enclosure. On the clothesline hung several pair of men's trousers, a few dark cotton dresses, and a row of towels, pinned in orderly fashion.

Eli put his hand against the small of Laura's back, leading her around the house and up the steps of a wide back porch. When they entered the kitchen, Laura's mouth fell open. She *had* stepped back in time—to the pioneer days.

The smell of sweet cinnamon and apples permeated the room, drawing Laura's attention to the black, wood-burning stove in one corner of the room. There were no curtains on the windows, only dark shades, pulled halfway down. Except for a small battery-operated clock and one simple calendar, the stark white walls were bare.

A huge table was in the middle of the kitchen. Long wooden

benches were placed on either side, and two straight-backed chairs sat at each end. A kerosene lamp hung overhead, with a smaller one sitting in the center of the table. Against one wall was a tall wooden cabinet, with a sink and a hand pump sandwiched on the sideboard. Strategically placed near a massive stone fireplace were a rocking chair and a well-used couch.

Like a statue, Laura stood near the door. "Do all Amish live this way?"

Eli moved across the room. "What way?"

"So little furnishings. There aren't any pictures on the walls and no window curtains. Everything looks so bare."

"Our religion doesn't permit such things," Eli explained. "The Old Order Amish believe only what serves as necessary is needed in the home. The Bible forbids God's people from makin' graven images."

Laura didn't have a clue what Eli was talking about. All she knew was this home was like no other she'd ever seen. Here was a group of people, living in the modern world, yet having so little to do with it. It was unbelievable!

Eli grinned when a slightly plump Amish woman entered the room. Her brown hair, worn in the traditional bun and covered with a small white cap, was peppered with gray. Her hazel-colored eyes held a note of question when she spotted Laura.

"Mom, I'd like ya to meet Laura Meade," Eli said quickly. He motioned toward Laura, then back to his mother. "This is my *mamm,* Mary Ellen Yoder."

She hates me. The woman's just met me, and I can tell by her expression that she's decided I'm the enemy. Laura forced a smile. "It's nice to meet you, Mrs. Yoder."

Mary Ellen moved toward the stove and began to stir the big pot of simmering apples. "Do ya live around here?"

"No—"

"Has your car broken down, or are ya just another curious tourist who wants to check out the strange people livin' in the plain house?"

"I'm none of those things, Mrs. Yoder. I'm from Minneapolis,

Minnesota, but I'm attending the Lancaster School of Design," Laura explained.

Mary Ellen whirled around, casting Eli a questioning look.

"We met at Farmers' Market a few weeks ago," he said. "Laura was interested in my birdhouses. I've been showin' her around."

Mary Ellen's gaze went to the wicker basket in Eli's hand. "You two have been on a picnic?"

"*Jah,* we went to Paradise Lake," he answered.

"It's beautiful there," Laura put in. "The lunch you made was wonderful."

Before Eli's mother could respond, the kitchen door flew open, and two young men sauntered into the room. They were speaking in their native tongue but fell silent when they saw Laura standing beside Eli.

"These are my younger brothers, Lewis and Jonas," Eli said, motioning toward the rowdy pair. "Boys, this is Laura Meade. We met at Farmers' Market."

Lewis nudged Jonas and chuckled. *"Es gookt verderbt schee doh!"*

Jonas laughed and nodded. *"Jah,* it does look mighty nice here!"

Laura felt the heat of a blush stain her cheeks. "It's nice to meet you."

Turning to his mother, Jonas said, "Pop'll be right in. How 'bout some lemonade? We've worked up quite a thirst."

Mary Ellen nodded and moved across the room to the icebox.

Jonas, who had light brown hair and blue eyes like Eli's, pulled out one of the benches at the table. "Why don't ya set yourself down and talk awhile?"

Laura glanced at Eli to see if he approved, but he merely leaned against the cupboard and smiled at her. His mother was already pouring huge glasses of lemonade.

Laura had the distinct feeling Mrs. Yoder would be happy to see her leave, and she was about to decline the invitation when

Eli spoke up. "We'd be glad to have a cold drink, and maybe some of those ginger cookies you made yesterday, Mom."

With a curt nod, Mary Ellen scooped several handfuls of cookies out of a ceramic jar. She piled them on a plate and brought them and the lemonade to the table.

Lewis and Jonas dropped to one bench, and Eli and Laura sat on the other one.

Eli made small talk with his brothers, and occasionally Laura interrupted with a question or two. She was getting an education in Amish culture that rivaled anything she'd ever read about or seen on any postcard.

The young people were nearly finished with their refreshments when the back door flew open. A tall, husky man with graying hair and a full beard lumbered into the room. He slung his straw hat over a wall peg, then went to wash up at the sink. All conversation at the table ceased, and Laura waited expectantly to see what would happen next.

The older man dried his hands on a towel, then took a seat in the chair at one end of the table. He glanced at Laura but said nothing.

❧

Eli decided he needed to break the silence. "Laura, this is my *daed*, Johnny Yoder. Pop, I'd like ya to meet Laura Meade."

Laura nodded. "Mr. Yoder."

Pop turned to Mom, who was now chopping vegetables at the kitchen sideboard. "What's to eat?"

Mom's face was stoic as she replied in Pennsylvania Dutch, "The rest are havin' lemonade and cookies. Do you want some?"

Pop grunted, "All right, I am satisfied."

Mom brought another pitcher of lemonade to the table and placed it in front of her husband.

"Danki," Pop muttered.

Eli turned to his father again. "Laura's from Minneapolis, Minnesota. She's attendin' some fancy school in Lancaster."

"The wisdom of the world is foolishness," Pop grumbled in his native language.

Eli shot him an imploring look. "There's no need to be goin' rude on my guest."

"Ah, so the Englisher can't understand the Dutch. Is this the problem?" Pop asked with a flick of his wrist.

"What kind of fancy school is it?" Lewis questioned.

"I'm learning to be an interior decorator," Laura answered.

"It's so's she can help folks decorate their homes real fancy-like," Eli interjected.

"It wonders me so that anyone could put such emphasis on worldly things," Mom commented while placing another plate of cookies on the table.

"Laura and I went to Paradise Lake for a picnic," Eli said, changing the subject to what he hoped was safer ground. "It sure is beautiful now. Some of the leaves are beginnin' to fall."

"I'll be glad when it's wintertime and the lake freezes over," Jonas added. "I love to go ice-skatin'."

Eli noticed that Laura's hands were trembling. He wasn't the least bit surprised when she hopped off the bench and announced, "Eli, I think I should be going."

He sprang to his feet as well. "I'm gonna drive Laura to The Country Store. I'll be back in plenty of time for chores and supper."

When no one responded, Eli jerked the back door open so he and Laura could make a hasty exit. "Well, that went well," he grumbled a few minutes later.

"I'm sorry for putting you through all that," she murmured as he helped her into the buggy. "Your family obviously doesn't approve of me."

"Don't worry about it. We're just friends."

"Your folks sure do talk funny," Laura commented.

"In the privacy of our homes, we often speak Pennsylvania Dutch," Eli explained.

Laura shook her head. "I wasn't talking about that."

"What then?" he asked, giving her a sidelong glance.

"Your mother said, 'It wonders me so,' and one of your brothers said, 'Set yourself down and talk awhile.' " Laura giggled. "That kind of talk sounds so uneducated."

Eli pulled sharply on the reins, guiding the horse to the side of the road. When the buggy came to a complete stop, he turned to face Laura. "Are you makin' fun of my family?"

"No, no, of course not," she stammered. "I just meant—"

Eli held up his hand. "You don't have to explain. I know how strange we Amish must seem to you English. We talk differently, dress differently, and *jah*, even think counter thoughts. It's who we are, and we don't care how the world chooses to view us."

Laura twisted the ends of her purse strap, biting down on her lower lip. "I–I'm sorry. I didn't mean to make light of the way you talk." She looked away. "Maybe it *would* be better if you never saw me again."

"No!" Eli was quick to say. He grabbed her hand. "I wanna be your friend. I'll be glad to show ya around more of our Amish villages whenever you like."

"Even if your parents disapprove?"

He nodded. "*Jah*, but I think I can make 'em see reason. Pop and Mom are really fun-lovin', easygoin' folks." He shrugged. "After all, we're not courtin' or anything. There's really nothin' for them to be concerned about."

Laura smiled sweetly. "How about next Saturday? Could you show me around then?"

He pursed his lips. "I think I could."

❧

Eli returned home in time for supper. He'd no more than taken his seat when the lectures began. "You play with fire, and you're bound to get burned!" Pop shouted. "There's always trouble somewhere, and that Englisher has trouble written all over her pretty little face."

Eli snorted and reached for a buttermilk biscuit. He ripped off a hunk and dipped it into his stew. "I've come of age. I should be allowed to make my own decisions. Don't you think it's time?"

Jonas grinned. "I'm thinkin' my big brother is *Asu Liebe*."

"I am not in love!" Eli snapped. "Laura and I are just friends. I don't see how it could hurt for me to spend a little time showin' her around the countryside and sharin' a bit about our Amish ways."

"The Amish ways? Why would she be needin' to know our ways?" asked Mom. "The English who come nosin' around our community are usually nothin' but trouble. It has always been this way."

"Laura's not trouble, Mom," Eli defended. "She's just curious about our lifestyle, and I think—"

"You are mixed up!" Pop roared. "A few questions here, and a few trips around the country there, and soon that foreigner will be tryin' to talk you into leavin' the faith."

Eli felt his face flame. "No way, Pop!"

"Eli's secure in the faith," Lewis interjected. "He got baptized and joined the church much younger than either Jonas or I did. Ain't it so, Jonas?"

Before Jonas could open his mouth, Pop hollered, "You'd best be stayin' outta this, boy. If ya can't keep your opinions to yourself, then you'll be doin' double chorin' for the next two weeks!"

Lewis fell silent. Eli, however, couldn't keep quiet. He swallowed the last bit of food in his mouth. "Are ya forbiddin' me to see Laura again?"

Pop shook his head. "No, all Amish *Yunga* have the right to choose. However, you're already a church member. You must be careful not to let anything cloud your judgment. As long as ya don't get *Asu Liebe* for the Englisher or let her tear ya away from the faith, we won't interfere."

"We don't have to like it, though," Mom added.

Eli stood up. "I think I'll go out to my workshop and do some carvin'." He made a hasty exit out the back door, ignoring the concerned looks exchanged among those left at the table.

❧

Laura collapsed onto her bed. She felt as if she hadn't slept in days. Today had been exhausting. By the time Eli had dropped her off in front of The Country Store, all her energy was zapped. Until today, Laura had usually been able to charm anyone she'd met. Not only had she not charmed Eli's parents, but she was quite sure she'd actually alienated them.

Laura knew she would have to take things slow and easy. She didn't want to scare Eli off by making him think there was more to their relationship than mere friendship. After all, that's all there really was at this point, but she was hoping for more—so much more.

four

Saturday dawned with an ugly, gray sky and depressing, drizzling rain. Laura groaned as she stared out the window of her dorm room. She figured Eli probably wouldn't show up for their rendezvous at all. If they went for another buggy ride, they'd be drenched in no time; and she seriously doubted that he'd want to pass the time sitting in some restaurant or wandering through a bunch of tourist-filled souvenir shops. They weren't supposed to meet until two o'clock, so with any luck, maybe the rain would be gone by then.

Laura turned from the window and ambled over to her desk, fully intending to get in a few hours of study time. Her mind seemed unwilling to cooperate, so she ended up pushing the books aside and painting her fingernails instead.

By noon, the drizzle had turned into a full-fledged downpour. Laura could only hope Eli Yoder would not stand her up.

૨ઢ

"From the way you're dressed, I'd say you're going out. What I want to know is where you're heading on an icky day like this."

Laura was watching out the downstairs window for her taxi, and she turned at the sound of Darla's voice. Laura offered a brief smile and held up her green umbrella. "I'm waiting for a cab to take me to the village of Paradise."

Darla's forehead wrinkled. "I thought you'd be up in your room studying. What do you want to do, drown in liquid sunshine?"

Laura laughed. "I can't concentrate on schoolwork today. Besides, I'm supposed to meet Eli at The Country Store."

Darla's frown deepened. "You may be gorgeous, but you sure don't have a lick of sense."

"What's that supposed to mean?" Laura moved away from

36

the window and began to pace the length of the hallway.

"It means you're barking up the wrong tree, chasing after that Amish fellow."

"It's none of your business."

Darla started toward the visitors' lounge. "Do whatever you want, but don't come crying to me when you get your delicate little toes stepped on."

A honking horn turned Laura's attention back to the window. "My taxi's here. I've gotta go. See you later, Darla."

❧

Laura stepped from the cab just in time to witness a touching scene. Eli Yoder was standing in front of The Country Store, holding a black umbrella over his head. The minute he spotted Laura, he stepped forward and, like a true gentleman, positioned the umbrella over her.

She smiled up at him, her heart pounding with expectation. "I'm surprised to see you."

"We said we'd meet here," Eli said with a friendly grin.

She nodded. "Yes, but it's raining, so I know we can't go for a buggy ride."

"We Amish don't stay home just 'cause it rains." Eli steered her across the parking lot. "I brought one of our closed-in buggies today."

Laura's heart was beating a staccato rhythm as she felt the warmth of his hand on her elbow, and she realized it was something she could easily become accustomed to.

Eli helped her into the gray, box-shaped buggy, then went around to the driver's side.

"Where are we going?"

"Is there anything in particular you're wantin' to see?"

She shrugged and leaned her head against the padded leather seat. Her heart felt light, and she was content just being with Eli, so it didn't really matter where they went.

"The farmers' market is open today," Eli said, breaking into her thoughts. "Would ya like to go there?"

She smiled. "I'd love to go to the farmers' market. There

are so many interesting things to see there."

"Jah," he agreed, "and today they're havin' a craft show, so many Amish and English will be sellin' their wares."

"It sounds like fun." Laura stole a glance at Eli. "Are you selling any of your wooden creations?"

"Himmel—I mean, no, no. I just want to look around today. Maybe get a few ideas 'bout what I might carve."

"Good idea." Laura smiled. "Maybe I'll get some more decorating ideas, too."

❧

They entered the farmers' market and found a host of people roaming up and down the aisles. *The rain sure didn't keep anyone at home,* Laura noted. *Apparently, folks from Lancaster Valley appreciate a craft show as much as Eli and I do.*

"Let's start over here," Eli suggested, directing Laura's attention to a table on their left.

What a strange-looking couple we must make, thought Laura when she noticed several people staring at them. *Eli, dressed in his plain Amish clothes, and me, wearing designer blue jeans and a fancy monogrammed sweatshirt.* "Well, let them stare," she murmured.

"What was that?" Eli asked, moving close to the table of a Mennonite man who was selling small wooden windmills.

Laura shrugged. "Nothing. I was talking to myself."

Eli let out a low whistle as he picked up one of the windmills. "Finely crafted—very fine."

"It's nice," Laura agreed.

"Are ya hungry? Want somethin' to eat or drink?" he asked when they moved on.

"No, but if you're hungry, I'll drink a diet soda and watch you eat."

Eli pinched her arm lightly. "A diet soda for someone so skinny?"

"I am not skinny," she retorted. "I'm merely trying to keep my figure."

Eli's ears turned red as he looked her up and down. "Your

figure looks right *gut* to me."

Laura giggled self-consciously. "Thanks for the nice compliment, but for your information, this shape doesn't come easy. I have to work at staying slender, and it means watching what I eat."

Eli raised his dark eyebrows as he continued to study her. "One so pretty shouldn't be concerned about gainin' a few pounds. Mom's pleasantly plump, and Pop says he likes her thataway."

Laura folded her arms across her chest. "You'll never catch me in any kind of plump state—pleasantly or otherwise."

Eli chuckled. "Someday you'll meet a great guy, get married, and have a whole house full of *kinder*. Then you won't even have a figure, much less have to worry 'bout keepin' it."

Laura flinched. "If I ever do get married, I have no intention of losing my shape!"

Eli steered her toward the snack bar at one end of the market. "I didn't mean to get your dander up. If ya ask me, you're way too touchy 'bout your weight."

"I don't recall asking you!" she snapped. "What would you know anyway? You're used to plain, fat women."

Eli jerked his head as though she'd slapped him across the face. "Maybe today wasn't such a *gut* idea after all. Maybe I should take you back to The Country Store."

Laura clutched at his shirtsleeve. "Please, Eli, can't we start over? I didn't mean to offend you."

They had reached the snack bar, and Eli turned to face her. "Our worlds are very different, Laura. I'm plain, and you're fancy. I see things differently than you do. I'm afraid it'll always be so."

Laura shook her head, her eyes filling with unwanted tears. "We're just getting to know each other. It's going to take a bit of time for us to understand one another's ways."

"Maybe we never will," he said with a frown. "I've been Amish all my life, and it's the only way I know."

She smiled up at him. "I can teach you modern things, and

you can teach me Amish ways. I really want to learn, and I promise to be more tactful."

"I guess we can give it another try." Eli tapped Laura on the arm. "Can I interest ya in a glass of root beer and a giant, homemade pretzel?"

Afraid of hurting his feelings or getting into another discussion about her weight, Laura nodded. "Sure, why not." After all, she could count calories on her own time.

❧

Laura lay on the bed, her mind replaying the events of the day. As strange as it might seem, she was glad she and Eli had experienced their first disagreement. In spite of the dissension it had caused, it actually seemed to strengthen their relationship. For the remainder of the day, Eli had been compromising, and she'd done the same.

A soft knock on the door stirred Laura from her musings. "Who is it?"

"Darla."

Laura crawled off the bed. Jerking open the door, she shot Darla a look of irritation. "If this little visit is going to be another lecture, you can save your breath."

Darla shook her head. "I wanted to apologize for this afternoon." She smiled brightly. "And see how your day went."

Laura motioned her inside. "Actually, it went well. Eli and I took in a craft show at Farmers' Market in Bird-in-Hand, and I got more decorating ideas."

Darla flopped onto the bed. "From what I've been told, the Amish don't believe in decorations or fancy adornments in their homes."

"True," Laura agreed, "but that's what makes it so unique."

"I don't follow."

Laura dropped down next to Darla. She ran her fingers across the quilt on her bed. "Take this, for example. It's plain, yet strikingly beautiful." She raised her eyebrows. "A quilt like this is in high demand, which is why it was so costly."

Darla shrugged. "To be perfectly honest, Amish decor

doesn't do much for me. Neither do Amish men."

Laura clenched her jaw. This conversation was leading to another argument, and she was not in the mood. "It's been a long day, and I'm dog-tired. Do you mind if we continue this discussion some other time?"

Darla stood up and started for the door. "I almost forgot—you had a phone call while you were out exploring Amish land."

"Who was it?"

"Mrs. Evans took the call, and all she told me was that it was some guy, asking for you."

"Hmm. . .maybe it was Dad."

"I really couldn't say, but I think Mrs. Evans left a note in your mailbox."

"I'll go check, thanks," Laura said, following Darla out.

Darla waved and disappeared into her own room, and Laura ran down the steps. She found the note in her mailbox, just as Darla said. It read: *A man named Dean Carlson called around two o'clock. He wondered why he hadn't heard from you lately and wants you to give him a call as soon as possible.*

Laura sucked in her breath. So Dean was missing her. *Do I call him first thing in the morning, or should I make him wait a few days?*

&

Laura held the phone away from her ear and grimaced. She knew she'd made a mistake calling Dean so early in the morning. She should have remembered he was a bear before his third cup of coffee.

"What do you mean, you don't want me to come to Lancaster for a visit?" he barked.

"It's not that I don't want you to come," she said sweetly. "It's just that—I'll be coming home for Christmas, and—"

"Christmas? That's three months away!"

"I know, but—"

"I'm flying in next weekend, and that's all there is to it."

"No, no, it's not a good idea."

"Why not?"

Laura could almost see Dean's furrowed brows and the defiant lift of his chin. He was a handsome man, with jet-black hair that curled around his ears and eyes as blue as a summer sky.

Laura twisted the end of the phone cord around her finger as she struggled to find the right words. "It would be great to see you, Dean, but I always have lots of homework on the weekends, and—"

"Were you studying yesterday when I phoned?"

Laura sucked in her breath, knowing she couldn't possibly tell Dean about her Saturday date with Eli Yoder. "I—uh, went to the farmers' market."

"What's that got to do with homework?" he growled.

"I was researching the Amish culture."

"You're kidding, right?"

"No, I've been studying their quilts and getting some ideas for my next designing project." *I've been studying a fascinating Amish man, too.*

Dean cleared his throat. "How about next weekend? Can I come or not?"

Laura chewed on her lower lip. She liked Dean. . .or at least she had when they were seeing each other socially. Why was she giving him the runaround now? It only took a few seconds for her to realize the answer. She was infatuated with Eli Yoder and wanted to spend her weekends with him. Dean would only be a distraction, and if Eli found out about her English boyfriend, it might spoil her chances of getting him to leave the Amish faith.

"Laura, are you still there?"

Dean's deep voice drew Laura back to their conversation, and she sighed deeply. "Yes, I'm here."

"What's it gonna be?"

"I'd rather you didn't come."

"Is that your final word?"

"Yes. As I said before, I'll be home for Christmas."

Dean grunted, said good-bye, and hung up the phone. Laura breathed a sigh of relief. At least one problem was solved.

five

Over the next several weeks, Eli and Laura saw each other whenever possible. In fact, Eli could hardly get Laura out of his thoughts. The vision of her beautiful face, smooth as peaches and cream, inched its way through his mind on more than one occasion. He had finally told his folks he was still seeing Laura, and the news hadn't gone over well, especially with Mom.

"She'll try to change you," she admonished one Saturday, as Eli was hitching the buggy for another trip to meet Laura. "Why, the first thing ya know, that English woman will be askin' you to leave the faith."

"*Ach,* Mom. No one could ever talk me into somethin' like that!"

Mom pursed her lips. "I wouldn't be so sure. Love does strange things to people."

Eli's eyebrows shot up. "Love? Who said anything about love, for goodness' sake?"

Mom gave him a knowing look. "I've seen the face of love before, Son. Every time ya come home after bein' with that fancy woman, I can see the look of love all over your precious face."

Eli felt himself blush. He would never admit it, especially not to Mom, but he was beginning to wonder if his fascination with Laura might be more than curiosity or friendship. What if he were actually falling in love with her? If she felt the same way about him, would she really expect him to leave the faith?

"Well, are ya headin' out or not?"

Mom's question drew Eli out of his musings. "*Jah,* I'm on my way."

As Eli stepped into the buggy, Mom waved. "Don't be too late, and remember what I said. We'd never live through a shunnin' in this family."

"There will be no shunnin'!" Eli called as he steered the horse down the driveway.

≥

Laura leaned her head out the buggy window and drew in a deep breath. "It smells like winter's coming!" she exclaimed.

Eli nodded. "I'm sorry it's so cold. Now we have to be content with one of Pop's closed-in buggies." He exhaled a groan. "I sure do miss my courtin' buggy."

"Don't you use it in the winter months at all?" she asked.

He shrugged. "Sometimes, on the milder days, but it's much warmer inside this buggy, don'tcha think?"

"*Jah,*" she said with a giggle and a flip of her ponytail.

Eli grinned. "You look mighty *schnuck* today."

"*Schnuck?* What's that?"

"It means *cute.*"

Laura's heart fluttered. "Thanks for the compliment."

Eli only nodded and made the horse go a bit faster.

"Where are you taking me today?" Laura asked.

"I thought ya might like to see one of our schoolhouses."

"Schoolhouses? You have school on Saturdays?"

He chuckled. "No, but Saturday's the best day for a tour of the schoolhouse. There won't be any *kinder* about, and no teacher wearin' a stern look or carryin' a hickory switch."

Laura shook her head. "Eli Yoder, you're such a big tease." She reached across the short span between them and touched his arm. "Maybe that's why I like you so well."

"Because I like to kid around?"

"Yes. I find your humor and wholesome view on life kind of refreshing. It's like a warm breeze on a sweltering summer day."

Eli scrunched up his nose. "I don't believe I've ever been compared to a warm breeze before."

She withdrew her hand and leaned back. "I've learned a lot from you."

"Is that *gut* or bad?"

"It's *gut,* of course." Her voice lowered to a whisper. "I could teach you a lot about English ways, if you'd let me. We could take in a movie sometime, or—"

Eli held up his hand. "No, thanks. I think I know more'n I need to know 'bout the fancy life."

"How can you say that? Have you ever given yourself a chance to find out what the modern world really has to offer?"

"I ain't blind, Laura," he muttered. "I see what's out there in the world, and I'm not the least bit interested in electrical gadgets, fancy clothes, or thinkin' I don't need God."

Laura's mouth dropped open. "Who ever said anything about not needing God?"

"I know some English folks do love God," Eli said, "but many are too self-centered to give Him anything more'n a few thoughts, and then it's only when they need somethin'."

"Where did you hear that?" she asked, her voice edged with irritation. Was this going to turn into a full-fledged disagreement? If so, she wasn't sure it was a good idea to give her opinion. After all, she was trying to appease, not aggravate, Eli.

Eli shrugged. "It don't matter where I got the notion. The important thing is, I'm content to be Amish, happy to be a child of God, and I don't need no worldly things to make me complete."

"My dad says religion is a crutch for weak men." The words were out before Laura even had time to think.

Eli pulled sharply on the reins and eased the horse and buggy to the side of the road. "Are you sayin' I'm a weak man?"

She turned to face him. "No, of course not. I just meant—"

"Maybe we've come too far," Eli said, his forehead wrinkling.

"Too far? You mean, we missed the schoolhouse?"

He shook his head. "Too far with this friendship we've been tryin' to build."

Laura's heart began to pound, and her throat felt like it was on fire. If Eli broke things off now, there would be no chance for them. She couldn't let that happen. She would not allow him to stay angry with her for something so ridiculous as a difference of opinion on religious matters.

She touched his arm again. "Eli, I respect your religious beliefs, but can't we just agree to disagree on some things?"

"It's kind of hard to have a friendship with someone when we keep arguin'."

She nodded. "I know, so let's not argue anymore. In fact, if it would make you feel better, I'll just sit here and listen to you narrate. How's that sound?"

He reached for the reins. "You're a hard one to say no to, Laura Meade."

She smiled. "I know."

&

It was only the first week of December, but the valley had been hit with a heavy blanket of snow. Laura figured it would mean the end of her enjoyable rides with Eli. . .at least until spring. She'd be going home for Christmas soon, so that would put an end to their times anyway. Leaving Eli, even for a few weeks, wasn't going to be easy. However, she'd promised her parents and friends she would be coming for the holidays. Besides, even if she stayed in Pennsylvania, Eli would spend Christmas with his family, and she, the fancy English woman, would never be included in their plans.

Laura stared out her dorm room window. If only she had some way to get in touch with Eli. If they could just meet somewhere for lunch.

She finally curled up on her bed with a romance novel, surrendered to the fact that this Saturday would be spent indoors, without Eli Yoder.

Laura had only gotten to the second page when a loud knock drove her to her feet. "Who's there?"

"Darla. Are you busy?"

Laura opened the door. "What's up?"

Darla was wearing a pair of designer jeans and a pink angora sweater. A brown leather coat was slung over one arm, and a matching cap was perched on top of her short, blond curls. "I thought I'd drive into Philly today. I still have some Christmas shopping to do, and only the big stores have what I want."

"You're going shopping today?"

Darla nodded. "I was hoping you'd come along."

"In this weather?" Laura gestured toward the window. "In case you haven't noticed, there's a foot of snow on the ground!"

Darla shrugged. "I'm sure most of the main roads have been cleared." She nudged Laura's arm. "I'll treat you to lunch."

Laura released a sigh. "Oh, all right." It wasn't the way she really wanted to spend the day, but it was better than being cooped up in her room.

≥∙

The ride to Philadelphia went well. They took the main highway, and just as Darla had predicted, it had been plowed and sanded. In spite of the weather, the stores were crowded with holiday shoppers.

Laura and Darla pushed their way through the crowds until they'd both purchased enough Christmas presents for everyone on their lists. Everyone except Eli. Laura wanted to get him something special, but since he lived such a plain life and was against worldly things, she couldn't find anything suitable.

They left the city around four o'clock, and by the time they reached the turnpike, it was snowing again.

"I know it's a little out of the way, but would you mind stopping at The Country Store on our way home?" Laura asked Darla.

"What for?"

"I want to get a Christmas present for Eli. I couldn't find anything appropriate in Philly, but I'm sure I can find something in Paradise."

Darla squinted her eyes. "I don't mind stopping, but I do mind what you're doing."

Laura looked away. "What are you talking about?"

"I can see no matter how much I've warned you, you've decided to jump into the deep end of the pool."

"Huh?"

"Don't be coy with me, Laura. I've warned you about the Amish, and you've forged ahead anyway. It doesn't take a genius to see you're head over heels in love with this Eli fellow."

"In love? Don't be ridiculous! Eli and I are just friends."

Darla gave the steering wheel a few taps with her gloved fingers. "Sure. . .whatever you say."

When they arrived in Paradise, The Country Store looked deserted. A sign in the window said they were open, so Darla parked her car, and Laura went in.

She soon realized that choosing a gift for an Amish man, even in a Plain store, wasn't going to be easy. There were shelves full of men's black felt hats, suspenders in all sizes, and a large assortment of white handkerchiefs. Laura wanted something more special than any of these things. It had to be something that would make Eli remember her.

She was about to give up when she spotted a beautiful set of carving tools. She paid for them and left the store feeling satisfied with her purchase. Now if she only had some way to get the gift to Eli.

When she returned to the car, Laura noticed the snow had turned to freezing rain.

"This isn't good," Darla complained as they pulled out of the parking lot. "I should have gone directly back to Lancaster and stayed on the main roads."

Laura groaned. "I'm sure we'll get back to the school in time for your favorite TV show."

"I wasn't thinking about TV," Darla snapped. "I'm concerned about staying on the road and keeping my car intact."

No sooner had she spoken the words than they hit a thick patch of ice. The car slid off the road, coming to a stop in the middle of a snowbank.

"Oh, great!" Darla moaned. She put the car in reverse and tried to back up. The wheels spun, but the car didn't budge. Darla tried several more times, but it was no use. They were stuck, and there was nothing they could do about it.

"Maybe we should get out and push," Laura suggested with a weak smile.

"And maybe I should call for help," Darla said, reaching into her purse for the cell phone. She started to dial but dropped it onto the seat with a moan.

"What's wrong?"

"It's dead." Darla opened the car door and got out. Laura did the same.

"Now we're really in a fix," Darla complained. "I should have checked my phone battery before we left Lancaster this morning."

"I guess it's my fault. If I hadn't asked you to go to Paradise—"

Laura stopped speaking when she heard the *clip-clop* of a horse's hooves approaching. "Do ya need some help?" a deep, male voice called out.

She whirled around, and her heartbeat quickened. Eli Yoder was stepping down from an open sleigh. "Are we ever glad to see you!" she cried.

As soon as Eli joined them, Laura introduced Darla. Then, offering Eli her best smile, she asked, "Would it be possible for you to give us a ride to Lancaster? We need to call a tow truck for Darla's car."

Eli surveyed the situation. "I can pull you outta that snowbank with my horse."

Darla shook her head. "You've got to be kidding!"

"My horse is strong as an ox," he asserted.

Darla shrugged. "Okay. Give it a try."

Laura and Darla stepped aside as Eli unhitched the horse and hooked a heavy rope from the animal's neck to the back bumper of Darla's car. He said a few words in Pennsylvania Dutch, and the gelding moved forward. The car lurched and was pulled free on the first try.

"Hooray!" Laura shouted with her hands raised.

Darla just stood there with her mouth hanging open.

"Why don't I follow you back to Lancaster?" Eli suggested.

"That way I can be sure that you don't run into any more snowbanks."

"Thank you," Darla said.

"Would it be okay if I rode in your sleigh?" Laura asked Eli. "I've always wanted to go on a sleigh ride." She smiled at him. "Besides, I have something for you."

His brows arched upward. "You do?"

She nodded. "I'll get it from Darla's car and be right back." Laura raced off before Eli had a chance to reply. When she grabbed Eli's gift from the car, Darla, already in the driver's seat, gave her a disgruntled look but said nothing.

Laura made her way back to where Eli waited beside the sleigh. After he helped her up, she pulled the collar of her coat tightly around her neck. "Brr. . . It's sure nippy out."

Eli reached under the seat and retrieved a colorful quilt. He placed it across her lap, and she snuggled beneath its warmth, feeling like Cinderella on her way to the ball.

Eli followed Darla's car back to Lancaster. When they arrived in front of their dorm, Darla got out and came over to the sleigh. "Thanks again, Eli. You sure saved the day!"

"I'm glad I happened to be in the right place at the right time," he replied with a warm smile.

Darla looked up at Laura, still seated in the sleigh. "Are you getting out or what?"

She shook her head. "You go on. I need to speak with Eli."

Darla shrugged and walked away.

Laura turned to face Eli. "I'm glad you came along when you did. I'm leaving for Minneapolis in a few days, and I didn't think I'd get the chance to see you before I left."

"I went to The Country Store this mornin'," Eli said. "You weren't there, so I thought maybe you'd already gone home for the holidays."

Laura frowned. If she'd had any idea Eli was going to venture out in the snow just to see her, she'd have moved heaven and earth to get to Paradise this morning. "I really didn't think you'd be coming," she said softly. "I guess fate must have wanted us to meet today after all."

Eli raised one eyebrow. "Fate? You think fate brought us together?"

She nodded. "Don't you?"

He shook his head. "If anyone brought us together, it was God."

"I have something for you," Laura said, feeling a bit flustered. She handed him the paper bag, and her stomach lurched with nervous anticipation. "Merry Christmas, Eli."

Eli opened the sack and pulled out the carving set. He studied it a few seconds, then his forehead wrinkled. "It's a nice gift—much better than the carvin' set I use now." He fidgeted, and Laura was afraid he was going to hand it back to her.

"What's wrong? Don't you like it?"

"It's *wunderbaar*, but I'm not sure I should accept such a gift."

"Why not?" she asked, looking deeply into Eli's searching blue eyes.

"I have nothin' to give you in return."

Laura reached for his hand and gently closed her fingers around his. "Your friendship is the only Christmas present I need. Please say we can always be friends."

Eli swallowed hard, and she watched him struggle for composure. Several seconds went by, then he offered her a grin that calmed her fears and warmed her heart. "*Jah*, I'd like us to always be friends."

six

Laura's first few days at home were spent thinking about Eli. When she closed her eyes, she could visualize his warm smile, little chin dimple, and those clear, blue eyes, calling her to reach out to him.

Ever since Laura had returned home, her mother had been trying to keep her occupied. "Why not join me for lunch at Ethel Scott's this afternoon?" she suggested one morning.

Laura was lying on the couch in the living room, trying to read a novel she'd started the day before. She set it aside and sat up. "I need to get my Christmas presents wrapped."

Mom took a seat next to Laura. Her green eyes, mirroring Laura's, showed obvious concern. "I'm worried about you, Dear. You haven't been yourself since you came home for the holidays." She touched Laura's forehead. "Are you feeling ill?"

Laura shook her head. "I'm fine. Just a little bit bored. I'm used to being in class every weekday."

"That's precisely why you need to get out of the house and do something fun." Mom tipped her head, causing her shoulder-length auburn hair to fall across her cheek. Even at forty-five, she was still lovely and youthful looking.

"Ethel's daughter Gail is home from college, and I'm sure she'd be thrilled to see you," Mom continued. "In fact, she'd probably get a kick out of hearing about that boring little town you're living in now."

Laura moaned. "Lancaster isn't little, and it sure isn't boring."

"The point is, you've been cooped up in this house for days. Won't you please join me today? It'll be much better than being home alone."

"I won't be alone," Laura argued. "Foosie is here, and she's all the company I need." She glanced at her fluffy, ivory-colored

52

cat, sleeping contentedly in front of the fireplace. "After I'm done wrapping gifts, I thought I might give Shannon a call."

Mom stood up. "I would think it would be Dean Carlson you'd be calling." She shook her finger at Laura. "Dean's called at least four times in the past two days, and you always find some excuse not to speak with him."

Laura drew in her bottom lip. How could she explain her reluctance to talk to Dean? "I'll be seeing Dean on Christmas Day. That's soon enough."

Her mother shrugged and left the room.

Laura puckered her lips and made a kissing sound. "Here, Foosie, Foosie. Come, pretty lady."

The ball of fur uncurled, stretched lazily, then plodded across the room. Laura scooped Foosie into her lap and was rewarded with soft purring when the cat snuggled against her white angora sweater. "I've missed you. Too bad cats aren't allowed in the dorm rooms at school. If they were, I'd take you back with me."

The telephone rang and Laura frowned. "Just when we were getting all cozy." She placed the cat on the floor and headed for the phone, sitting on a small table near the door. "Meade residence."

"Laura, is that you?" a familiar female voice asked.

"It's me, Shannon."

"When did you get home?"

"Last Saturday."

"And you haven't called? I'm crushed."

Laura chuckled. "Sorry, but I've been kind of busy." *Busy thinking about Eli Yoder.*

"Is it all right if I come over?"

"Sure, I'd like that."

After Laura hung up the phone, she headed for the kitchen. She had two cups of hot chocolate ready by the time her friend arrived.

"Have a seat, and let's get caught up," Laura said, handing Shannon a mug.

Shannon sniffed her drink appreciatively. "You got any marshmallows?"

Laura went to the cupboard to look, while Shannon placed her mug on the table, then took off her coat. "I think it's gonna be a white Christmas. I can smell snowflakes in the air."

Laura tossed a bag of marshmallows on the table and took the seat across from Shannon. "We've already had a good snowstorm in Lancaster."

"Really? Were you able to get around okay?"

"Oh, sure. In fact, I—"

"Say, you haven't said a word about my new hairstyle," Shannon cut in. She dragged her fingers through her bluntly cut, straight black hair. "Do you like it?"

Laura feigned a smile as she searched for the right words. "You—uh—look different with short hair."

Shannon blew on her hot chocolate, then reached inside the plastic bag and withdrew two marshmallows. She dropped them into the mug and grinned. "I kind of like my new look."

"I'm surprised you would cut your hair. I thought you'd always keep it long."

Shannon shrugged, then took a sip of her drink. "Long hair is too much work, and it takes forever to dry." She set the cup down and snapped her fingers. "I know! Why don't you make an appointment at Brenda's Beauty Boutique and get your hair cut and styled while you're home for Christmas?"

Laura trembled at the thought of losing her shining glory. "I don't think I could ever cut my hair. It took me too long to get it this way."

Shannon poked at the marshmallows with the tip of her finger as she studied Laura. "Have you met any cute guys out there in Lancaster County?"

Laura smiled. "Eli Yoder. I sent you an E-mail about him."

"You mean that Amish fellow?"

"He's the one."

"I thought that was just a passing fancy. Surely you're not really interested in this guy."

Laura felt the heat of a blush creep up the back of her neck and spread quickly to her face. "I've been fighting my attraction to Eli, but it's a losing battle." She drew in a deep breath and let it out in a rush. "To tell you the truth, I think I might be in love with him."

Shannon nearly choked on her hot chocolate. "You can't be serious!"

"I am."

Shannon leaned forward, as though she were sharing some dark secret. "Does he know how you feel?"

"I don't think so. We've only agreed to be friends, and I don't see how it could work for us to have a romantic relationship."

Shannon nodded. "Makes sense to me."

"Eli's really religious," Laura remarked. "We're worlds apart, with him being a plain kind of guy, and me being a fancy English woman." She laughed dryly. "At least that's how Eli sees me."

Shannon drummed her fingers along the edge of the table. "Hmm. . ."

"What?"

"Maybe he'll leave the Amish faith and become *fancy.*"

"I've thought about that—even hoped for it," Laura admitted. "I think it's just wishful thinking, though. Eli's religion and his plain lifestyle are very important to him. I doubt he'd be willing give to it up, though I am going to ask—when I get the nerve."

Shannon reached across the table and patted Laura's hand. "This is a fine fix you've got yourself into. Maybe you'll end up going over to the other side before it's all said and done."

Laura's eyebrows furrowed. "Other side? What are you talking about?"

"I was thinking you might join the Amish faith. People have done a lot stranger things in the name of love."

Laura's frown deepened. "I don't think I could do that, Shannon. It would be so hard to give up everything I have, and—"

The kitchen door flew open, chopping off Laura's sentence. Her father entered the room, carrying an overstuffed briefcase and frowning like there was no tomorrow. From the way his shoulders were sagging, and the grim look he was wearing, Laura figured he must either be exhausted or terribly agitated about something.

Dad was a small, thin man, with dark brown hair and a matching mustache. His mahogany eyes looked unusually doleful as he shuffled across the room and collapsed into a chair.

"Dad, is something wrong?" Laura asked with concern. "You look so tired."

"It's just this fast-paced world we're living in," he answered, lowering his briefcase to the table. "On days like today, I wish I could pull a magic handle and make everything slow down. Maybe the pioneer days weren't so bad. Life in the fast lane is pretty hectic, but I suppose I'll survive." He pursed his lips and looked right at Laura. "Whatever you do, young lady, never let 'all work and no play' become your motto."

Dad's words made Laura think of Eli and his Amish family. They worked hard, but they weren't living in the fast-paced world. They took time for fun and relaxation. She wondered if Dad were given the chance, whether he might trade in his briefcase for a hoe and the quiet life among the Plain People. She chucked softly. *Naw, that could never happen.*

&

Eli meandered toward his woodworking shop at one end of the barn. He didn't know why, but he wasn't in the mood to carve or build one single thing.

He looked down at the woodworking set Laura had given him and groaned. He wished she hadn't presented him with such a fine, expensive gift. In fact, he wished she hadn't bought him anything at all. He'd given her nothing in return, and accepting Laura's present only made it that much harder to distance himself from her.

Eli sank to the metal folding chair by his workbench and

leaned forward, until his head was resting in the palm of his hands. "If only I hadn't told her we could always be friends. It just ain't right."

"What ain't right?"

Eli jerked upright at the sound of his younger brother's voice. "Jonas, what do ya think you're doin', sneakin' up on me thataway?"

Jonas chuckled and sauntered over to the workbench. "I thought you came out here to work on a Christmas present, not talk to yourself," he said, giving Eli's shoulder a good smack.

Eli frowned. "I was plannin' on finishin' up the planter box I'm makin' for Martha Rose, but I can't seem to get in the mood."

Jonas pulled a bale of straw over to the bench and plopped down on it. "Christmas is only a few days away. How do ya think our big sister will feel 'bout not gettin' a gift from you?"

Eli grabbed the planter in question, along with a strip of sandpaper, and began sanding it with a vengeance. "It'll be done on time."

Jonas touched Eli's arm. "Take it easy. You're gettin' all worked up."

"I ain't worked up," Eli snapped as he continued to run the coarse paper over the edges of the wooden box.

Jonas eyed Eli intently. "Is that so? Well, ya sure could've fooled me."

"Quit starin'!" Eli shouted.

"I was just checkin' to see if my big brother is *Asu Liebe*."

Eli slapped the sandpaper down on the bench and stood up, nearly knocking over his chair. "I ain't in love! Now, if ya don't have nothin' sensible to say, why don'tcha get on outta here?"

"It's that fancy English woman, ain't it so?"

Eli's forehead was beaded with sweat, and he knew it wasn't from heat, for there was at least a foot of snow on the ground. If only he could get Laura out of his mind. . .

"You're not denyin' it, so it must be true," Jonas persisted. "She's gotten under your skin, huh?"

Eli whirled around to face his brother. "Laura and I are just friends." His eyelid began to twitch. "Even if I wanted it to be more, it could never happen."

"How come?"

"She's English."

"I know, but—"

"There's no buts," Eli said impatiently. "I'd never leave our faith, and I sure couldn't ask Laura to become one of us."

"Why not?"

Eli folded his arms across his chest and drew in a deep breath. He was getting mighty frustrated with his little brother and this ridiculous conversation they were having. "Let's put it this way—would ya throw a newborn baby kitten into the pigpen?"

Jonas looked at him as if he'd gone daffy. "Huh? What's a little bitty kitten got to do with Laura Meade?"

Eli shook his head. "Never mind. You're probably too *ver-huddelt* to understand."

"I'm not mixed up! Just say what ya mean, and mean what ya say!" Now Jonas's forehead was dripping with sweat.

"Calm down," Eli commanded. "This is a dumb discussion, and I say we drop it."

Jonas elevated his chin defiantly. "Ya know what I think?"

Eli blew out his breath and lifted his gaze toward the rafters. "No, but I'm sure ya won't scram 'til you've told me."

"I think you're in love with Laura Meade, but ya know she's no good for you. I'm thinkin' the best thing for everyone is for you to hurry and get hitched up with Pauline Hostetler."

Eli clenched his fists. If Jonas didn't leave soon, he couldn't be sure what he might do. With a trembling finger he pointed to the door. "Just go—now!"

❧

Christmas Day turned out to be pretty much the way Laura had expected. Her father invited several people from his law firm to dinner, and most of them spent the whole time talking about trial dates, briefs, and who they thought might get out of going to jail.

Among the guests was Dean Carlson, seated right next to Laura. She studied him as he droned on and on about the new computer system they'd recently installed at the office. There was no denying it—Dean was handsome. The funny thing was, Laura used to enjoy Dean's company. Now he seemed superficial and self-absorbed. She kept comparing him to Eli, whose warm, sincere smile could melt her heart, and whose infectious laughter was genuine, not forced like Dean's. She didn't know why she'd never seen it before, but Dean's whole mannerism was brash, and he was certainly the most egotistical man she'd ever met. Eli, on the other hand, was gentle and genuinely humble.

"Laura, are you listening to me?" Dean asked, breaking into her private thoughts.

She managed a weak smile. "I think Dad may have mentioned the new computer system."

"You *weren't* listening," he snapped. "The computer system was not the last thing I said."

She blinked. "It wasn't?"

"I was asking if you'd like to go to the New Year's Eve office party with me."

Laura stared at Dean. How could she even consider dating a man like him? Oh, sure, he had money, a good education, and a prestigious job, but he simply wasn't Eli Yoder.

"I want to take you to the party," Dean said again. "Will you go or not?"

Every fiber of her being shouted *"Not!"* She reached for her glass of water and took a few sips, hoping to buy some time.

When Dean began tapping the side of his glass with the tip of his spoon, she finally answered. "I appreciate the offer, but I hadn't planned on going to the party this year."

"Why not?"

Laura wasn't sure how to respond. She really had no legitimate reason for staying home. "I—uh—I'm leaving for Pennsylvania the day after New Year's, and I need to get packed."

Dean leaned his head back and roared. It was the first genuine laugh she'd heard out of him all day, but it didn't make her smile. "You have a whole week between now and the party. Surely that's time enough to pack a suitcase."

When Laura made no reply, he reached for her hand. "Come on, Honey, please say you'll go with me. After all, I do work for your dad, and I know he would approve."

Laura groaned inwardly. She knew she was losing this battle, and she didn't like it one bit. "Well, I—"

Dean leaned closer, and she could feel his warm breath against her ear. "If you don't have a wonderful time, I promise never to ask you out again."

Laura nodded in defeat. "Okay, I'll go."

❧

Mom had insisted Laura buy a new dress for the party. She couldn't understand what the fuss was about but decided she might as well enjoy the pampering. After all, she'd be leaving soon, then it would be back to the grindstone of school, homework, and. . .Eli. She hoped she could figure out a way to meet him again.

Standing before her full-length bedroom mirror, Laura smiled at the lovely young woman looking back at her. *If Eli could only see me now.*

Mom stood directly behind her, and she smiled into the mirror as well. "You look exquisite. I'm glad you decided to buy this beautiful silk gown. That shade of green brings out the color of your eyes so well."

Laura merely shrugged.

"I'm sure Dean will be impressed," her mother continued. "He's such a nice man."

"I suppose—just not my type."

"Not your type?" Mom's eyebrows furrowed. "How can you say that, Laura? Why, Dean is nice looking, has plenty of money, and—"

Laura turned away from the mirror. "Do you think my hair looks all right this way, or should I have worn it down?"

"Your hair looks lovely in a French roll," her mother responded. She gave Laura's arm a gentle squeeze. "I'm sure Dean will think so, too."

❧

The New Year's Eve party at the country club was already in full swing when Dean and Laura arrived. He'd been nearly an hour late picking her up, which had put her in a sour mood right from the beginning.

They'd no sooner checked their coats, when Dean pulled her into a possessive embrace. "You look stunning tonight, Laura. I'm so glad you decided to come."

Laura wished she could reciprocate with a similar remark, but the truth was, she wasn't glad to be here. In fact, she felt a headache coming on, and if it didn't let up soon, she knew she'd have a good excuse to leave the party.

"Would you like something to drink before we check out the buffet?" Dean asked.

She merely shrugged in response.

"What can I get you from the bar?"

"Nothing, unless they have diet cola."

"You're not driving," Dean reminded. "And if you're concerned about me drinking and driving, you shouldn't worry your pretty little head. I can handle a few drinks without any problem at all."

Laura gnawed on her bottom lip until it almost bled. If Dean was planning to have a few drinks, she could only imagine how the evening might end. She had to do something to get away from him now. "There's my friend, Shannon," she said. "I'm going over to say hi."

"Okay, I'll get our drinks, then I'll meet you at the buffet table in ten minutes." He sauntered off toward the bar.

Laura saw Shannon carrying her plate to one of the tables. "I'm glad to see you here," she said, taking a seat beside her friend.

"Why wouldn't I be?" Shannon asked. "My boyfriend, Clark, does work for your dad, you know." She glanced at the buffet table. "Clark's still loading up on food, but he'll b joining me soon."

Laura shrugged. If Shannon's comment was meant to cha her away, it wasn't going to work. "Listen, can you do me big favor?" she asked.

"If it's within my power."

"I'm gonna call a cab and go home, so when Dean com looking for me, would you tell him I had a splitting headac and left?"

"Tell him yourself. He's heading this way." Shannon pointe across the room, and Laura groaned.

"What's wrong? Did you two have a little disagreement?"

"Something like that." Laura decided it would be pointle to tell her friend the real reason she wanted to get away fro Dean Carlson. The truth was, she wasn't just worried abor his drinking. She didn't like that gleam in his eyes tonigh She was sure he wanted more than she was willing to give.

"Here's your diet cola," Dean said, handing Laura the col drink. He nodded at Shannon. "How's it going?"

Shannon smiled. "Fine. How's everything with you?"

Laura set her glass on the table and tuned them both out : they engaged in small talk. Her thoughts turned naturally t Eli, and she couldn't help wondering how he was spendin his New Year's Eve. She cringed when Dean pulled he thoughts away. "Tonight's going to be a great evening," h said, stroking the back of her neck.

She stood up quickly, knocking her soft drink over, an spilling some of it down the front of her new dress. "I–I'r not feeling well, Dean. I'm going to call a cab and go home.'

Dean's eyebrows furrowed. "You can't be serious. We ju got here, and I haven't had a chance to eat yet, much le show you off to my friends."

I don't want to be shown off. Laura thrust out her chin an looked at him defiantly. "I'm going home!"

"Okay, okay, don't get yourself in such a huff," Dean sai set his drink on the table and steered her toward the coa closet. "I'll get my car."

"I'm calling a cab," she insisted. "There's no point in both of us missing the party. You stay and have a good time."

He smiled, and his eyes clouded over. "If you're dead set on going, then I may as well collect that stroke of midnight kiss." Before Laura could say anything, Dean bent his head and captured her lips in a kiss that would have left most women reeling with pleasure.

Laura drew back and slapped his face.

"What was that for?" he barked, reaching up to touch the red mark on his cheek. "I thought you wanted that kiss as much as I did."

Laura's face was so hot, she felt as though she were the one who'd been slapped. She wasn't in control of her emotions tonight, and that really bothered her.

"I'm sorry, Dean," she apologized. "Your kiss took me by surprise."

Dean's eyelids fluttered and he backed up a few steps. "I don't know what's come over you, Laura, but you haven't been the same since you left Minneapolis to attend that stupid school in Pennsylvania. If I were your father, I would never have allowed you to go there and would have insisted you finish your designing courses right here in town."

Laura's hands were trembling as she held them at her sides. If Dean kept goading her, she was liable to let him have it on the other cheek. "Good night, Dean," she said through clenched teeth. "Don't bother walking me out."

seven

The day after New Year's, Laura said good-bye to her parents at the airport. She was more than anxious to be on her way. It wasn't that she hadn't enjoyed being with them, but she wanted to get back to her studies. . .and Eli Yoder.

Laura hugged Mom and Dad, thanking them for the beautiful leather coat they'd given her for Christmas. Then, without so much as a backward glance, she boarded the plane, welcoming the butterflies doing a tap dance in her stomach.

Her time on the plane was spent sleeping and thinking about Eli. Laura couldn't decide if she should be straightforward and tell him that she'd come to realize how much she loved him, or if she should be coy, hoping to draw a declaration of love from him first.

By the time the plane landed in Philadelphia, she was a ball of nerves. The next flight to Lancaster wasn't for two hours, and she didn't relish the thought of sitting around the airport that long. If there hadn't been snow on the ground, she might have considered renting a car and driving to Lancaster.

She became absorbed in her newest romance novel but felt relief when the boarding call finally came. She still hadn't figured out how, but by this time tomorrow, she would have bared her soul to Eli.

⁂

Laura awoke in her dorm room the following morning with a pounding headache. A warm shower and a cup of tea helped some, but when she knocked on Darla's door to ask for a ride to Eli's farm, Laura's headache worsened.

"I have other plans today," Darla informed her. "Besides, I wouldn't even consider being a party to you ruining your life."

"How can seeing Eli ruin my life?"

Darla opened the door wider and motioned Laura inside. "Have a seat and I'll see if I can explain things to you."

Laura pulled out the desk chair, and Darla sat on the edge of her bed.

"I know you've got a thing for this guy, but the more you see him, the further your relationship will develop." Darla pursed her lips. "One of you is bound to get hurt, and it's my guess, you're gonna be the one."

"What makes you think I'll get hurt?"

"We've been through this before. You and Eli are from different worlds, and even if one of you were dumb enough to try the other's way of life, it wouldn't work."

"How do you know?"

"Trust me on this," Darla asserted. "You're living in a dream world if you think you can ever get Eli to leave his faith."

"Why is that so impossible?" Laura snapped. "People change religions all the time."

"If Eli turns his back on the Amish church, he'll be shunned. Do you understand what that means?"

Laura nodded and her throat tightened. "Eli has told me quite a bit about the Amish."

"Then you know how serious it is when someone leaves the faith and becomes part of the modern world."

"That will have to be Eli's decision." Laura stood up. "If you're not available to drive me to the Yoder farm, then I'll call a cab."

⁂

Laura stepped out of the taxi and walked carefully up the slippery path leading to the Yoders' front porch. She was almost to the door when a sense of panic gripped her. What if Eli wasn't home? What if he was home but wasn't happy to see her?

It was too late to turn around, for the cab was already out of sight. Laura knocked on the door.

A few moments later, Mary Ellen Yoder answered. She was holding a rolling pin in one hand, and with the other hand she swiped at a wisp of hair that had fallen loose from her bun. Laura couldn't read the woman's stoic expression, but her silence was enough to remind her that she was on enemy territory.

"Is Eli at home?"

"He's out in the barn, workin' in his wood shop," Mary Ellen said in a cool tone.

Laura gritted her teeth and forced herself to smile. "Thanks; I'll go find him." She stepped quickly off the porch, before Eli's mother had a chance to say anything more. If the older woman's sour expression was meant to dissuade her, it hadn't worked. Laura was here now, and she was more determined than ever to speak with Eli.

⁂

Eli was bent over his workbench, hammering a nail into the roof of a small birdhouse, when he heard the barn door open. He didn't think much of it, knowing his brothers were still busy with chores; but when a familiar female voice called out to him, he was so surprised, he smashed his thumb with the hammer.

"Laura? What are you doin' here? How'd ya get here?"

Slowly, she moved across the room, until she stood right in front of Eli. "I came in a cab. I had to see you."

"When did you get back from Minnesota?"

"Last night."

Eli wished she would quit staring at him. It was hard to think. Hard to breathe. He swallowed a couple of times. "How was your holiday?"

"It was okay. How was yours?"

"Gut," he answered. *Though it would have been better if you'd been here.* Eli shook his head, trying to get himself thinking straight again.

"I've missed you," Laura said, leaning into him. "Did you miss me?"

A warning went off in Eli's head, but it was too late. Laura's hand was on his arm, and she was gazing into his eyes in a way that made his heart slam into his chest. How could he tell her it wasn't right for her to be here?

Eli couldn't voice any of his thoughts. In fact, he couldn't even think straight with her standing there so close and smelling so nice. "Paradise Lake is completely frozen now. Would ya like to go ice-skating?" he asked suddenly.

She tipped her head slightly. "Ice-skating? Eli, I have no skates."

He grinned. "I think my sister left her skates here in the barn when she married Amon Zook."

Laura smiled. "If your sister's skates fit, I'd be happy to go ice-skating."

❧

Paradise Lake was covered with a thick layer of shimmering ice. Laura thought it was even more appealing than it had been in the fall. She drank in the beauty of the surrounding trees, dressed in frosty white gowns and shimmering in the morning sun like thousands of tiny diamonds.

Eli helped her into his sister's skates, which were only a tad too big. Hand in hand, they skated around the lake. Then Eli set off on his own, doing fancy spins and figure eights.

Laura shielded her eyes against the glare of the sun as she watched in rapt fascination, realizing with each passing moment how much she loved Eli Yoder. She tried skating by herself, but it was hard to concentrate on anything but the striking figure he made on the ice. He was wearing a pair of black pants, a light blue shirt, and a gray woolen jacket. He'd removed his black felt hat, and his sandy brown hair whipped against his face as he appeared to become one with the wind.

Laura's heart hammered in her chest when Eli waved and offered her a flirty wink. She tried to catch up to him, hoping they could take a break and sit awhile. They needed to talk. She needed to tell him what was in her heart.

Pushing off quickly, Laura lost her balance and landed hard on the ice. Eli was at her side immediately, his blue eyes looking ever so serious. "Are you okay? Ya didn't break anything, I hope."

"My knee hurts, but I don't think my leg's broken."

Laura winced as Eli pulled up her pant leg to examine the injury. "It looks like just a bad bruise," he remarked. "You probably should put some ice on it."

"I think I just did," she said with a giggle.

Eli helped Laura to her feet and over to the sleigh. "I'd better get you back to your school so you can rest that knee."

Laura gripped Eli's shoulders and, standing on tiptoes, she kissed him on the cheek.

He smiled at first, then jerked back like he'd been stung by a bee. "What was that for?"

"Just my way of saying thanks for being such a *gut* friend."

His blue eyes grew serious. "I—I think it'd be best if we didn't see each other anymore."

"Why?" Laura cried. "Haven't you enjoyed yourself today?"

He nodded soberly. *"Jah,* that's the problem."

Her chin quivered slightly. "I don't see how enjoying yourself can be a problem."

"I told you once we could always be friends, but now things have changed."

"How?"

"I can't be your friend, because I've fallen in love with you, Laura."

"Oh, Eli!" she exclaimed. "I love you, too!" She buried her face in his jacket, relishing the warmth and his masculine smell.

"What we feel for each other ain't right," Eli mumbled.

"It sure feels right to me."

"It won't work for us," he insisted. "We have to end this before we both get hurt."

"Nothing could hurt worse than never seeing you again," Laura said with a catch in her voice. "We can be together if we want it badly enough."

He eased her gently away. "I don't see how."

"You could leave the Amish faith. We'd be able to date then. When we both feel ready, we could get married, and—"

Eli's eyebrows arched. "Married? Are ya saying you'd marry me?"

Laura swallowed. Is that what she was saying? Did she really love Eli, or was he simply a prize she wanted and thought she couldn't have?

"In time we might be ready for marriage," she amended.

Eli shook his head. "I could never leave the Amish faith or move away from God. Please, don't ask me to do that."

She grasped his coat collar. "I'm not asking you to leave God. You can worship Him in any church. I'm only asking you to give up your Plain lifestyle, with all its silly rules." She leaned close to him again. "I know you'd be happier if you could do a few worldly things. Won't you at least give it some thought?"

Eli stepped away from her, then motioned toward the sleigh. "It's time to go. This discussion is over."

Laura's eyes filled with tears as he helped her into the sleigh. When he picked up the reins and they began to move forward, she felt as though her whole world was falling apart. "Eli, you never said. Will you think about my proposal?"

He looked straight ahead.

"Please, don't shut me out. Won't you give our relationship a chance?" she pleaded.

Eli remained silent all the way back to Laura's school. When he stopped at the front gate, he came around to help her down. She clung to him, but he pushed her gently away. "Good-bye, Laura."

Tears of frustration trickled down her cheeks. Why wouldn't Eli listen to reason? What had gone wrong with her plan?

❧

January and February were cold. . .so cold and dreary Laura thought she would die. It wasn't just the weather making her feel that way. Her heart was broken because Eli had rejected her. If he really cared, he should have agreed to leave his rigid faith and join the "real" world. Two months had passed since their final good-bye, but Laura still longed for something she couldn't have. Visions of the happy times they'd spent together danced through her mind. Losing Eli hurt so much, and she couldn't do anything to ease the pain. Shopping for clothes didn't help. Throwing herself into her studies made no difference. Even an occasional binge on hot-fudge sundaes and chocolate milkshakes did nothing to make her feel better. The barrage of E-mails and phone calls from Dean Carlson didn't soothe Laura's troubled spirit, either. She cared nothing for Dean, and she told him so.

As winter moved into spring, Laura moved on with her life. At least she thought she was moving on, until one of her teachers gave the class an assignment, asking each student to decorate a bedroom, using an Amish quilt as the focal point.

Laura had her own Amish quilt. . .the one she'd purchased at the farmers' market, the first day she'd meet Eli. When she and Eli broke off their relationship, she'd sent it home. She supposed she could call Mom and ask her to mail it back, but this assignment was due next week, and there would hardly be enough time for that. There was only one logical thing to do—go to the farmers' market and buy another quilt.

❧

Laura was glad Darla had agreed to join her this time. She didn't relish the idea of going to Farmers' Market alone. There were too many painful memories there. Too many reminders of Eli.

Darla parked her car, and they went inside the building. A normal Saturday would have been busy at the market, but there weren't many tourists in Lancaster Valley yet, so the majority of people were just local shoppers.

"I'm beginning to see why the country look fascinates you," Darla said as they browsed through a stack of colorful quilts. "The vibrant hues and various shapes in these comforters are actually quite pretty."

Laura nodded as she fingered a monochromatic blue quilt with a double-wedding-ring pattern. "I think I'll buy this one.

I love the variance of colors and the interlocking rings."

"I think I'll keep looking awhile. No sense picking the first one I see," Darla said with a chuckle. When Laura didn't answer, she poked her in the ribs. "Did you hear what I said?"

Still no reply.

Laura stood frozen in her tracks. Her heart was pounding like a pack of stampeding horses, and her throat felt so dry she could barely swallow.

"Laura, what's wrong? You look like you've seen a ghost."

"It's Eli—and that woman," Laura said, her voice cracking. "I had no idea he would be here today. If I'd known, I sure wouldn't have come."

"Where is he, and what woman are you talking about?" Darla asked.

"She's Eli's girlfriend, and they're right over there." Laura pointed toward the root beer stand several feet away. "I shouldn't be surprised to see them together, but it still hurts."

Darla grabbed Laura's arm. "Come on. We've gotta get you out of here."

Laura jerked away. "I'm not going anywhere. This is a free country, and I have as much right to be here as they do."

"I'm sure, but you don't want Eli to know you're here. Do you?"

Laura hung her head. "Maybe."

"What? The guy threw you over for some Plain Jane, and you want to grovel in the dirt in front of him?"

"He didn't throw me over, and I wasn't planning to grovel. I was just thinking I should say hello."

"Now that's a brilliant idea." Darla turned back toward the stack of coverlets. "You do whatever you like, but I came here to look at Amish quilts. That *was* our assignment, you know."

Laura took a deep breath, glanced back at her friend, then marched straight up to Eli.

"Laura? What are you doing here?" he asked with a look of surprise.

"I'm looking at quilts," she answered, fixing her gaze

somewhere near the center of his chest. "I have an assignment to do, and—"

"Come on, Eli, let's go," Pauline Hostetler interrupted. She gave his shirtsleeve a good yank, then glanced over at Laura, bestowing her with an icy stare.

Laura's hands were shaking badly, and tension pulled the muscles in her neck. She had a deep sense she'd done the wrong thing asking Eli to leave his faith, and she couldn't ignore it a moment longer.

She took a guarded step forward. "Eli, could we talk? I need to tell you something." Her mouth went dry with trepidation. She stared into his deep blue eyes and recognized his hesitation.

He shrugged. "*Jah,* I guess it'd be all right." He glanced over at Pauline. "Could ya wait for me at your folks' table? I won't be long."

Pauline hesitated, then stalked off, muttering something under her breath.

"Should we go outside?" Eli suggested.

Laura followed as he led the way to the nearest exit. When they stepped out, he motioned toward a wooden bench near the building.

Once she was seated, Laura felt a bit more comfortable. At least now she could gulp in some fresh air, which she hoped might tame the brigade of bumblebees marching through her stomach.

"What did ya wanna talk about?" Eli asked.

"Us. I wanted to talk about us."

"There is no *us,* Laura," he said, shaking his head. "I thought you understood I can't leave my faith."

"I do understand, Eli," she said softly. "I'm sorry for asking you to give up your way of life."

Eli's lips curved into a smile. "Someday you'll meet the right man, and—"

Laura covered his mouth with her fingers. "I've already found the right man."

His eyebrows raised in obvious surprise. "You have? That's *gut*. I wish you all the best."

She compressed her lips in frustration. Was Eli deaf, dumb, and blind? Couldn't he see how much she wanted him? She grasped both of his hands and gave them a squeeze. "The man I've found is you, Eli. I want no other, and I never will."

"But, Laura—"

"I know, I know. You can't leave the Amish faith and become a fancy Englisher." She swallowed hard and took a deep breath. "That doesn't mean we can't be together, though."

He looked at her as if she'd lost her mind. "It don't?"

She shook her head. "I can come over to the other side."

"I'm afraid I don't get your meanin'," he said, a deep frown creasing his forehead.

"I'll join the Amish faith and become Plain."

"You don't know what you're sayin', Laura," he whispered. "A few folks have joined our faith, but not many. It ain't easy, ya know."

"I'm sure it's not," she agreed, "but I can do it, Eli. I can do anything for you."

Eli couldn't believe Laura was offering to join his faith. During the time they'd been seeing each other, he'd often found himself wishing for such a miracle, but she'd asked him to join her in the fancy world. Now she wanted to become Plain? It made no sense at all. He studied her intently. She seemed sincere, but truth be told, Laura didn't have any idea what she was suggesting. "I do love you, and I probably always will," he acknowledged.

"I'm so glad to hear that," she said, leaning closer and placing her hand on his arm. "I was afraid you might turn me away."

Eli breathed in the strawberry scent of Laura's hair and reveled in the warmth of her touch. How could he make her understand, yet how could he say good-bye again?

"These last few months have been awful," Laura asserted.

"I need to be with you."

Eli's voice shook with emotion. "You might not be happy bein' Amish. It would be a hard thing to change over and give up all the modern, worldly things you've become used to havin'. You'd have to learn our language and accept our religious views."

She nodded. "I know it won't be easy, but with your help, I can do it. You will help me, won't you, Eli?"

Filling his lungs with fresh air and struggling to make a decision, Eli lifted Laura's chin with his thumb and stared into her sea green eyes. They were meant for each other. He knew it in his heart. He pushed aside the niggling doubts. Nothing could go wrong. Laura would just need some time to adjust. *"Jah,* I'll help in every way I can," he murmured.

eight

Once Laura made her decision to become Amish, everything in her life changed as quickly as a leaf falls from a tree. The purchase of a second quilt had been forgotten when she decided to go back to the interior design school and withdraw. Next, she called her parents and told them what she had done. They were understandably shocked, and her mother threatened to fly right out to Pennsylvania to talk some sense into Laura. Her father seemed almost too understanding. Laura wondered if he wanted her to be happy, or if it was possible that Dad could actually identify with her desire to go Plain.

Laura would be living with Eli's sister, Martha Rose, so she gave her mother the address and asked her to send the quilt she'd originally purchased.

When they hung up the phone that afternoon, Laura's mother reminded her that she could always come home if things didn't work out. Laura figured her parents probably thought this was a lark—something she'd try on like a new pair of shoes, and when she decided they weren't to her liking, she would discard them. That was likely the reason they'd accepted her decision as well as they had.

"Be happy, Laura, and please keep in touch," were Dad's final words.

⁂

Eli was glad his sister had agreed to let Laura stay there, and even happier that Martha Rose was willing to mentor his fancy English woman who wanted to become Plain. Mom and Pop were another matter. They were no more thrilled about the idea of Laura joining the Amish faith than they had been about Eli seeing her when she was still English. It was hard to understand how Mom, who normally was so pleasant and easygoing, seemed almost rude to Laura when she'd visited their home. Even now, with her about to become Amish, there was a coolness in the way his mother spoke to Laura. He hoped things would change once Laura took her training and was baptized into the faith.

><

Martha Rose and Amon Zook lived in a typical Amish home. There were four bedrooms upstairs, and the one Laura was given was closest to the bathroom. For this, she was grateful, even though it didn't take long for her to realize there wouldn't be much time for primping or leisurely bubble baths. In fact, with only one bathroom in the house, she would have to hurry through her daily regime to allow others the use of the "necessary room."

When Eli's sister showed Laura her room, she was shocked. It was even smaller than her dorm room at the school had been. And plain. . .so very plain. There was a double bed, a chest of drawers with a washbowl and pitcher sitting on top, and a small cedar chest at the foot of the bed. Dark shades hung at the two windows, and, except for a small, braided throw rug, the hardwood floor was bare. Instead of a closet, her clothes would be hung on wooden pegs, connected to a narrow strip of wood along one wall.

"Here's a few dresses you can wear," Martha Rose said, handing Laura two long, cotton frocks. One was dark blue, the other a drab green. "You're a bit shorter than me, so they might be kinda long." She grinned. "Better too long than too short."

Laura stood there, too dumbfounded to speak. In her excitement to join the Amish faith and win Eli's heart, she'd forgotten that she would be expected to wear such colorless, outdated clothing. She glanced over at Martha Rose. She had a lovely face—creamy complexion, dark brown eyes—and it was framed by hair the color of chestnuts. She was tall and large-boned, but certainly not fat. *She could be a beautiful woman if she didn't have to hide behind such plain clothes and that drab hairdo.*

"I have a white head coverin' and also a dark bonnet for you to wear," Martha Rose continued. "And you'll need a few aprons."

Laura nodded mutely as she was given the rest of her new wardrobe. *What have I gotten myself into?* She inhaled deeply and drew from her inner strength. She could do this. Her determination and love for Eli would see her through anything.

"We'll go to The Country Store tomorrow and buy you some black leather shoes for church and other special occasions," Martha Rose announced. "If you already own a pair of sneakers, you can wear them for every day." She looked down at her own bare feet and smiled. "Of course, most of us just go barefoot around home, especially during the warmer weather. It saves our shoes, and it's much cooler."

Laura shifted uneasily. Barefoot? Sneakers and black leather shoes? Were those her only choices? In her new wardrobe, she would no doubt feel like a little girl playing dress-up. "Don't your feet get pretty dirty and sore, running around barefoot?" she questioned.

Martha Rose nodded. *"Jah,* but they toughen up, and we always wash our feet before goin' to bed."

Laura shrugged. What could she really say? She'd gotten herself into this predicament, and it was of her own choosing that she'd decided to go Plain. She would simply draw from her inner strength and do whatever was necessary in order to convince Eli and his family she was worthy of being part of their clan. After she and Eli were married, then she could ask again if he would consider leaving the Amish faith and join the "real world."

🍂

The next few days were busy. . .busier than Laura ever imagined. She had so much to learn about cooking, sewing, baking, doing laundry and other household chores, not to mention the terrible outside jobs. Gathering eggs, slopping the hogs, and cultivating the garden were all things she'd never done before. It was dirty, backbreaking work, and she made so many foolish mistakes.

One morning, as Laura was getting dressed, she glanced at herself in the hand mirror she'd stuffed in the chest of drawers, along with her satchel of makeup. For some reason, she just couldn't part with these things, so she hadn't mailed them home with all her clothes.

Today was Saturday, and Laura knew Eli would be coming to take her for a buggy ride. They planned to go into Paradise and do some shopping, then stop for a picnic on the way home.

Laura stared longingly at the tube of lipstick she held in her hand. *What would it hurt to apply a little color to my pale lips? If I don't do something to keep myself attractive, Eli might lose interest in me and go back to Pauline.*

Laura blended the coral lipstick with the tips of her fingers, then reached inside the makeup case for some blush. A little dab blended on each cheek and she looked less pale. She added a coat of mascara to her eyelashes and filled in her brows with a soft cinnamon pencil.

"There now," she whispered to her reflection. "I almost look like my old self—not nearly so dowdy." She glanced down at her plain green dress and scowled. "What I wouldn't give to put on a pair of jeans and a T-shirt." She slipped her head covering on and sighed. "Guess I'd better get used to all this. . .at least until Eli and I are married. Then I'll have the freedom to do as I choose."

Downstairs in the kitchen, Laura found Martha Rose and Mary Ellen sitting at the table drinking a cup of tea and eating shoofly pie. Just the smell of the molasses-filled pastry made Laura's stomach churn. No matter how long she was forced to stay Amish, she didn't think she would ever acquire a taste for this particular dessert.

"Gut Morgen," Martha Rose said cheerfully, when Laura joined them at the table.

"Gut Morgen to you, too," she responded with a slight nod. Learning Pennsylvania Dutch was another challenge for Laura, along with studying the Bible and learning the church

rules, which the Amish called *Ordnung*.

Mary Ellen studied Laura intently. "What's that you've got on your face?"

Laura shrugged and reached for an apple from the ceramic bowl in the center of the table. "Just a little color to make me look alive," she mumbled as she bit into the succulent fruit.

"Makeup's not allowed," Eli's mother persisted. "Surely you know that."

Laura looked pointedly at Mary Ellen, challenging her with her eyes. "I think it's a silly rule. What harm can there be in trying to make yourself a bit more attractive?"

" 'Favour is deceitful, and beauty is vain: but a woman that feareth the Lord, she shall be praised,' " Mary Ellen quoted.

Laura squinted her eyes. "Where'd you hear that?"

"It's in the book of Proverbs," Martha Rose answered, before her mother had a chance to respond.

"*Jah,* that's true," Mary Ellen agreed. She looked right at Laura. "Face powder may catch some men, but it takes bakin' powder to hold him."

Martha Rose giggled, and her mother chuckled behind her hand, but Laura sat there stony-faced. She didn't see what was so funny. Besides, she had the distinct impression these two Plain women were laughing at *her.*

Laura pushed her chair away and stood up. She realized that among the Amish, women all looked pretty much the same. "I'll go wash the makeup off." *But I don't have to like it,* she added silently.

❧

Eli whistled as he hitched his horse to the open buggy. He was looking forward to his date with Laura, but he still couldn't believe she'd actually agreed to become Plain. She was beautiful, talented, and smart. He was sure she could have any man she wanted, yet it was him she'd chosen. Him and his Amish way of life.

"I'll make her happy," he mumbled. The horse whinnied and nuzzled the back of Eli's arm.

"At least *you* ain't givin' me a hard time," Eli remarked. "If Mom and Pop had their way, I'd be courtin' Pauline."

Eli knew his parents had his best interests at heart, but they didn't understand how much he loved Laura.

"It just ain't right, her bein' so fancy and all," Mom had said the day he'd given them the surprising news.

"*Jah*," Pop had agreed. "It's not gonna be easy for her to give up all the modern things she's been used to and start livin' as we do."

"Laura wants this," Eli had insisted. "She knows what she's givin' up, and it's her decision to do so. Won'tcha please give her a chance?"

His folks had agreed, but he was sure it was only to please him. Deep in his heart, Eli felt they were just waiting to say, "I told you so."

Eli climbed into the driver's seat and gathered up the reins. He knew Mom had gone over to Martha Rose's this morning, so she'd be seeing Laura even before he did.

He clucked to the horse and it moved forward. "Let's just hope things went well between Laura and Mom," he muttered. "If they didn't, I'm likely to have a cross woman on my hands the rest of the day."

৵

When Laura greeted Eli at the back door, he thought she looked like she'd lost her best friend. "What's wrong? Aren't ya happy to see me this mornin'? Do you still wanna go to Paradise, then on a picnic?"

"I do want to go, Eli, but—well, I'll tell you about it on the ride to town," she whispered.

Eli glanced at his mother and sister, sitting at the kitchen table. Mom merely shrugged, and Martha Rose offered him a weak smile.

"Would ya like to come in and have a piece of shoofly pie?" Mom asked.

Eli licked his lips and started across the room.

"I think we should be on our way," Laura said, stepping

between Eli and the table.

He frowned. "What's your hurry?"

"I've got quite a bit of shopping to do, and we don't want to get to the lake too late." She rushed past him, pulled a dark blue sweater from the wall peg by the back door, and grabbed the wicker picnic basket sitting on the cupboard.

Eli looked at Laura, standing by the door, tapping her foot. He glanced back at the table, and his mouth watered just thinking about how good a hunk of that pie would taste.

As though sensing his dilemma, Martha Rose said, "Why don'tcha take a few pieces along? You and Laura can have it with the picnic lunch she made."

Eli shrugged. "*Jah,* okay. I guess I can wait that long to sample some of your *gut* cookin', Sister."

He reached for the pie, but Martha Rose was too quick for him. She'd already begun slicing it by the time he got to the table. "If you really wanna help, get some waxed paper from the pantry," she instructed.

He did as he was told, not caring in the least that his big sister was bossing him around. He'd grown used to it over the years. Besides, she really didn't mean to sound so pushy. Martha Rose was and always had been a take-charge kind of person. She was pleasant and kind, so he could tolerate a little ordering about now and then.

"You two have a *gut* day," Martha Rose said as Eli and Laura started out the back door.

"*Jah,* and be sure to be home in time for chorin' and supper," Mom called.

"I will," Eli said, closing the door behind them.

Laura stopped at the bottom of the stairs, and Eli nearly ran straight into her. "What'd ya stop for? I could have knocked ya to the ground."

She scowled at him. "You're henpecked. Do you know that?"

His eyebrows furrowed. "You don't know what you're sayin', Laura."

Her nose twitched and she blinked her eyes. "Those two women have you eating out of the palms of their hands."

Eli started walking toward his open buggy. "They do not. I just happen to like pleasin' them, that's all. I love Mom and Martha Rose, and they're both mighty good to me."

"Well, they're not so good to me!"

Eli whirled around to face Laura. She looked madder than one of Pop's mules when a big old horsefly took a bite out of its ear. "How can ya say they're not good to you? Martha Rose took ya in, didn't she?"

Laura opened her mouth, but before she could respond, Eli rushed on. "She gave ya some of her dresses to wear, took ya shoppin' for shoes and the like, and both she and Mom have taken time out of their busy days to teach ya about house-keepin', cookin', Bible readin', and so many other things you'll be needin' to know before ya can be baptized."

Laura's lip protruded as she handed Eli the picnic basket. "I should've known you wouldn't understand. You're one of *them*."

"What's that supposed to mean?" Eli asked as he climbed into the buggy and took up the reins.

Laura was still standing on the other side of the buggy with her arms folded. "It means, you're Amish, and I'm not. I'm still considered an outsider, and I don't think any of your family will ever accept me as anything else."

"Of course they will." He glanced at her out of the corner of his eye. "Are ya gettin' in or not?"

"Aren't you going to help me up?"

He groaned. "I might have, if ya hadn't been naggin' at me. Besides, if you're gonna be Amish, then you'll need to be learnin' how to get in and out of our buggies without any help."

Laura was so angry she was visibly shaking. In fact, if she hadn't been sure she'd be forced to work all day, she would have turned around and marched right back to the house. It would serve Eli Yoder right if she broke this date!

"Time's a-wastin'," Eli announced.

She sighed deeply, lifted her skirt, and practically fell into the buggy.

Eli chuckled, then snapped the reins. The horse jerked forward, and Laura was thrown against her seat. "Be careful!" she cried. "Are you trying to throw my back out?"

Eli's only response was another deep guffaw, which only angered her further.

Laura smoothed her skirt, reached up to be sure her head covering was still in place, then folded her arms across her chest. "I'm glad you think everything's so funny! You can't imagine what I've been through these past few weeks."

"Has somethin' bad happened?" Eli's voice was laced with obvious concern, and he reached over to gently touch Laura's arm.

She moaned. "I'll say."

"What was it? Did ya get hurt? How come I didn't hear about it?"

She shook her head. "No, no, I wasn't hurt. At least not in the physical sense."

"What then?"

"I've nearly been worked to death every day since I moved from the Lancaster School of Design to your sister's house. It seems as though I just get to sleep and it's time to get up again." She frowned. "And that stupid rooster crowing at the top of his lungs every morning sure doesn't help things, either."

"Pop says the rooster is nature's alarm clock," Eli said with a grin.

How can he sit there looking so smug? Laura fumed. *Doesn't he care how hard I work? Doesn't he realize I'm doing all this for him?*

"In time, you'll get used to the long days," Eli maintained. "Someday you'll come to find pleasure in that old rooster's crow."

"Humph! I doubt that!" She held up her hands. "Do you realize that every single one of my nails is broken? Not to mention embedded with dirt I'll probably never be able to

scrub clean? Why, the other morning, Martha Rose had m
out in the garden, pulling weeds and spading with a rusty ol
hoe. I thought my back was going to break in two."

"You *will* get used to it."

She scrunched up her nose. "If I live to tell about it."

nine

Laura's days at the Zook farm flew by. As spring quickly turned into summer, each day became longer, hotter, and filled with more work. Instead of "becoming used to it," she found herself disliking each new day. How did these people exist without air-conditioning, ceiling fans, and swimming pools? How did the women stand wearing long dresses all summer, when they would have been so much cooler in a pair of shorts?

Laura had seen Amon and little Ben play in the creek near their home, and she longed to join them. Anything to get cooled off and have some real fun. Eli's mother's idea of fun was going to a quilting party or making shoofly pies.

To make matters worse, Laura had to attend church every other Sunday and sit with the women on unyielding, wooden, backless benches. She couldn't visit with Eli until the three-hour service was over, lunch had been served, and everything was cleaned up. The women waited on the men, of course, and they did all the cleaning, too. If Laura ever thought life as an Amish woman was going to be easy, she'd been sorely mistaken. On days like today, she wondered if she'd made the biggest mistake of her life by asking to join the Amish church.

"It's not too late to back out," she muttered as she set a basket of freshly washed laundry on the grass underneath the clothesline. "I can go back to the school in Lancaster. Better yet, I can go home to Mom and Dad in Minneapolis. At least they don't expect me to work from sunup to sunset every day but Sunday."

Laura heard a pathetic *mooo,* and she looked up to see several black-and-white cows lining the fence, a few feet from where she stood. They were swishing their tails. . .and looking right at her.

"Just what I need—a cheering section. Go away, cows! Get back to the field, grab a hunk of grass, start chewing your cuds, then go take a nice, long nap." She bent down, grabbed one of Amon's shirts, gave it a good shake, then clipped it to the clothesline. "At least you bovine critters are allowed the privilege of a nap now and then. That's more than I can say for any of the humans who live on this farm!"

"Maih gayn fa di kee?" a small voice asked.

Laura looked down. There stood little Ben, gazing up at her with all the seriousness of a three year old. He'd said something in Pennsylvania Dutch, but she had no idea what he was talking about. She'd been studying the Amish dialect for a few months, but there were still many unfamiliar words.

"Maih gayn fa di kee," the child repeated. This time he pointed toward the cows, still gawking at Laura like she was free entertainment.

"Ah, the cows. You're talking about the cows, aren't you?" she said, dropping to her knees beside the little boy. *"Maih gayn fa di kee."* Laura smiled. "We go for the cows!"

Ben looked up at her and grinned. *"Jah."* He really was a cute little thing, with his blond, Dutch-bobbed hair, big blue eyes, and two deep dimples framing his smile.

"The clothes are washed," Laura said in Pennsylvania Dutch. She pointed to the heap of laundry in the basket, hoping the change of subject would take the boy's mind off cows that couldn't be let out of the corral, no matter how much he may have wanted it.

Ben studied the basket a few seconds, then he frowned.

"Was ist letz—what is wrong?" she asked.

"Es hemm mitt en loch," he said, grabbing one of his daddy's shirts.

Laura smiled when she realized that the child was telling her about his father's shirt with a hole. She patted the top of Ben's head. "No doubt that shirt will end up in *my* pile of mending."

Ben made no comment, but then, she knew he couldn't understand. He would be taught English when he started school. With an impish grin, the boy climbed into the basket of wet clothes.

Laura was about to scold him, but Ben picked up one of his mother's dark bonnets and plunked it on top of his head. She sank to her knees and laughed so hard she had tears running down her face. The cows on the other side of the fence mooed, and the little boy giggled.

Maybe life on this humble, Amish farm wasn't all bad.

☙

Laura sat at the kitchen table, reading the Bible Martha Rose had given her. Why did it seem so confusing? She'd been to Sunday school and Bible school a few times when she was growing up. She'd even managed to memorize some Bible passages, in order to win a prize. Why couldn't she stay focused now?

"You've been at it quite awhile. Would ya like to take a break and have a glass of iced tea with me?" Martha Rose asked, pulling out a chair and sitting beside Laura.

Laura looked up and smiled. She really did need a break. "Thanks, I'd like that."

Martha Rose poured two glasses of iced tea and piled a plate high with peanut butter cookies.

"Are you trying to fatten me up?" Laura asked when the goodies were set on the table.

Martha Rose chuckled. "As a matter of fact, you are pretty thin. I figured a few months livin' with me, and you'd have gained at least ten pounds."

Laura shrugged. "Your cooking is wonderful, but I'm trying to watch my weight."

"You need to eat hearty in order to keep up your strength," Martha Rose chided. She pushed the cookie plate in front of Laura. "Please, have a few."

Laura shrugged. "I guess two cookies wouldn't hurt."

"How are your studies comin' along?" Martha Rose asked. "Has little Ben been stayin' outta your way?"

"He's never been a problem," Laura answered honestly. "In

fact, your little boy is a real sweetheart."

"*Jah,* well, he can also be a pill." Martha Rose shook her head. "Only this mornin' I found him playin' in the toilet, of all things. Said he was goin' fishin', like he and his pa did last week."

Laura laughed and shook her head. "Where is the little tyke now?"

"Down for a nap. I'm hopin' he stays asleep awhile, 'cause I've got a bunch of ripe tomatoes waitin' to be picked. Not to mention fixin' supper and gettin' a bit more cleanin' done. Church will be here this Sunday, ya know."

"I'd almost forgotten. Guess that means we'll have to do more cooking than normal," Laura said, already feeling the ache in her back from standing long hours at the stove.

Martha Rose shook her head. "Not really. Most of the women bring something to share, so I'll mostly be responsible for beverages and a big pot of bean soup."

"Isn't it kind of hot for soup?"

"We enjoy soup most any time of the year, and my *daed* always says, 'a little somethin' hot on the inside makes the outside heat seem much less.'"

Laura's brows knitted together. The Plain folk sure did have a funny way of looking at things. She wondered if she would ever truly feel a part of them.

Maybe I won't have to, she mused. *After Eli and I are married, I might be able to convince him to leave the Amish faith. Once I'm his wife, he'll have to listen to me. After all, I just read in the Bible this morning that husbands are supposed to love and nurture their wives. If Eli truly loves me, then he should be willing to do anything to make me happy.*

"How's the Pennsylvania Dutch comin'?" Martha Rose asked, breaking into Laura's thoughts.

"Not so good. I can understand more now, but I'm still having trouble speaking the words right."

"Practice makes perfect," Martha Rose said. "I think it might help if we spoke less English to you."

Laura nearly choked on the piece of cookie she'd just put in her mouth. "You're kidding."

"I think you need to hear more Dutch and less English. It'll force ya to study harder and try sayin' more words yourself."

Laura groaned. Wasn't it enough that she was being made to wear plain, drab clothes, labor all day on jobs she hated, conform to all kinds of rules she didn't understand, and get along without modern conveniences? Must she now be forced to speak and hear a foreign language most of the time?

As if she could read her thoughts, Martha Rose reached over and patted Laura's hand. "You do wanna become Amish, don'tcha?"

Tears welled up in Laura's eyes. "I love Eli, and I'd do anything for him, but I never dreamed it would be so hard."

"You say ya love my brother, but what about your love for God? It's Him you should be tryin' most to please, not Eli."

Laura swallowed hard. How could she tell Martha Rose that, while she did believe in God, she'd never really had a personal relationship with Him? She wasn't even sure she wanted one. After all, what had God ever done for her? If He were on her side, then wouldn't Eli have been willing to leave his religion and become English? They could have worshiped God in any church.

"Laura?" Martha Rose prompted.

She nodded. "I do want to please God. I just hope He knows how hard I'm trying and rewards me for all my efforts."

Martha Rose frowned. "We should never have to be rewarded for our good deeds or service to God. We're taught to be humble servants, never prideful, never wantin' more. There's joy in lovin' and servin' the Lord, as well as others."

Laura thought on that a few seconds. The Amish people she was living among did seem to emanate a certain kind of peaceful, joyful spirit. She couldn't figure out why, since they did without so many things.

Martha Rose pushed away from the table. "I think we should end this discussion and get busy pickin', don't you?"

Laura eased out of her chair. While she had no desire to spend the next few hours out in the hot sun, bent over a bunch of itchy tomato plants, at least she wouldn't be forced to hear any more of Martha Rose's lectures. Unless, of course, the woman decided to carry the conversation with them into the garden.

❧

Laura wasn't looking forward to another long, boring church service, but the promise of a "singing" that night gave her some measure of joy. It would be held in the Beachys' barn, and Eli had promised to take her. Since he'd be coming to Amon and Martha Rose's for preaching, he would probably stick around all day, then later escort Laura in his courting buggy to the singing.

As much as Laura hated all the chores she was expected to do, and didn't care for the way she was forced to dress, she never got tired of spending time with Eli. In fact, the more they were together, the more she was convinced she'd done the right thing by asking to become Amish. Even though Eli could get under her skin at times, he made her feel loved, nurtured, and happy. He treated her with respect—nothing like Dean Carlson had when they were dating.

Laura rarely thought about Dean anymore, and when she did, it was only to compare him to Eli. She did think about her parents, though. She wrote letters whenever she found time, but wished she had her computer so she could type a quick E-mail instead of writing everything in longhand. She'd even managed to call them a few times, when she went to town and could use a pay phone.

Mom and Dad were doing fine, but she knew they missed her. She was also aware that neither of them understood her decision to become Amish. Dad was the most indulgent, since he admittedly wished for a simpler life. Mom, on the other hand, thought the whole idea of living like the pioneers was utterly foolish. Whenever they talked, she always reminded Laura that she could come home.

"I'm not going home until Eli is ready to come with me,"

Laura muttered as she dressed for church that morning. "If things go as planned, I should be baptized into the Amish church sometime next month, then Eli and I will get married in November." She slipped into her dark blue dress. "If I have my way, we'll be living in Minneapolis by Christmas."

≥a

Eli felt a mounting sense of excitement over his date with Laura tonight. They'd been on plenty of other dates, but tonight he planned to kiss her.

Guess I really shouldn't be plannin' such a thing, he thought as he helped Laura into the buggy. Even though he'd told her awhile back that she should learn to get in by herself, he had decided to act gentlemanly tonight. He didn't want their date to end up in an argument, like it had a few other times this summer. Truth be told, he was a bit worried that Laura might not take to the Amish way of life, and if she were displeased with him, it could be that she'd leave—head straight back to that fancy school in Lancaster, or worse yet, go home to Minnesota.

"I've been looking forward to tonight," Laura murmured as she settled against the buggy seat.

"Jah, me too," Eli agreed. He glanced over at her and smiled. "You're sure pretty, ya know that?"

Laura lifted her hand to touch her head covering. "You really think so?"

He nodded. "I do."

"But my hair's not long and beautiful anymore," she argued.

Eli frowned. "Your hair's still long. You're just wearin' it up in the back now."

"I know, but it looks so plain this way."

He reached over to gently touch her arm. "You may become one of us Plain folk, but you'll never *be* plain, Laura."

She shrugged her shoulders. "I'll always feel plain wearing long dresses that don't even fit me right. And I miss not wearing makeup. I look so pale without lipstick, blush, and eye shadow."

Eli clicked his tongue. "You're a very *Shee Meedel*, with or without makeup."

Laura gave him a satisfied smile. "Thanks. I'm glad you think I'm a pretty girl."

❧

When they arrived at the Beachy farm, the barn was already filled with young people. The huge doors were swung open wide, allowing the evening breeze to circulate and help cool the barn.

Soon the singing began, and the song leader led the group in several slow hymns, followed by a few faster tunes. There were no musical instruments, but the singsong chant of voices permeated the air with a pleasant symphony of its own kind. Even Laura got caught up in the happy mood, and she was pleasantly surprised to realize she could actually follow along without too much difficulty.

When the singing was done, the young people paired off and the games began. Laura was breathless by the time she and Eli finished playing several rounds of Six-Handed Reel, which to her way of thinking was similar to square dancing.

"Would ya like a glass of lemonade and some cookies?" Eli asked as he led Laura over to one of the wooden benches along the wall.

She nodded. "That sounds wonderful. I mean, *wunderbaar.*"

Eli disappeared into the crowd around the refreshment table, and Laura leaned her head against the wooden plank behind her. She caught a glimpse of Pauline Hostetler, who appeared to be watching her.

It wasn't hard to see that Pauline was not fond of Laura. In the months since she'd been part of the Amish community, Pauline hadn't spoken one word to her. *She's jealous because Eli loves me and not her.* Laura knew it probably wasn't right, but she felt a sense of pleasure knowing she'd won Eli's heart. Someday he would be all hers.

"Here ya go," Eli said, handing Laura a tall glass of cold lemonade. "I was gonna get us some cookies, but the plate was empty. I didn't wanna wait around 'til one of the Beachy girls went to get more."

"That's okay," Laura said, flashing him a smile. "I ate a few too many of your sister's peanut butter cookies earlier this week, and I don't want to gain any weight."

Eli frowned. "You could use a few extra pounds."

Why? So I can end up looking like your slightly plump mother? Laura didn't vocalize her thoughts. Instead, she quietly sipped her lemonade. They'd be going home soon, and she didn't want to say anything to irritate Eli, for tonight was the night she planned to give him a *real* kiss.

ten

"If you're ready to go home now, I'll get the horse and buggy," Eli told Laura after they'd finished their refreshments.

She smiled. "I'm more than ready."

Eli offered her a quick wink. "I won't be long. Come outside when you see my horse pull up in front of the barn." He chuckled. "No point in us both gettin' bit up by all the swarmin' insects out tonight." He strolled out the door, leaving Laura standing by the refreshment table alone. She caught sight of Pauline, who exited the barn only moments after Eli had.

"She'd better not be looking for my man," Laura muttered under her breath.

"Were you speakin' to me?" a pleasant, female voice asked.

Laura whirled around and was greeted with a friendly smile from a young woman about her age, whom she'd seen before but never personally met.

"I was talking to myself," Laura admitted, feeling the heat of a blush creep up her neck.

The other woman nodded. "I do that sometimes." She extended her hand. "My name's Anna Beachy, and you're Laura, right?"

"Yes, I live with Martha Rose Zook and her family."

"I know. Martha Rose and I are *gut* friends. Have been since we were *kinder*." Anna's green eyes gleamed in the light of the kerosene lanterns hung from the barn rafters. "Our moms were friends when they were growin' up, too."

Laura nodded mechanically. While this was interesting trivia, she was most anxious to get outside and see if Eli had the buggy ready. What was taking him so long, anyway?

"Yep, our families have been linked together for quite a spell," Anna continued. "Martha Rose's *mamm*, Mary Ellen, is the stepdaughter of Miriam Hilty. The dear woman's gone on to heaven now, but Miriam, who everyone called 'Mim,' was a real *gut* friend of Sarah Stoltzfus, Rebekah Beachy's mother. Rebekah is my *mamm,* and she's partially paralyzed. She either uses a wheelchair or metal leg braces in order to get around. Has since she was a young girl, I'm told." Anna drew in a deep breath and rushed on. "Now, Grandma Sarah is livin' with my aunt Nadine, and—"

Anna's voice droned on and on, and Laura tapped her foot impatiently, wondering how she could politely excuse herself. "I see," she said in the brief seconds Anna came up for air. "It does sounds like you have a close-knit family." She cleared her throat a few times. "It's been nice chatting with you, Anna, but Eli's outside getting his horse and buggy ready to take me home. I'd better not keep him waiting."

"*Jah,* okay. You go ahead," Anna said cheerfully. "Tell Eli I said hello, and let him know he should inform his big sister she owes me a visit real soon."

"I'll be sure he gets the message." Laura hurried away before Anna could say anything more.

Once outside, she headed straight for the long line of buggies parked alongside the Beachys' barn. She stopped short when she saw Eli. He was talking to Pauline Hostetler!

❧

Eli backed against the buggy when Pauline reached up and stroked the side of his face. What was going on here? This didn't set well with him at all. Didn't Pauline know he was courting Laura Meade?

"That English woman will never make you happy, Eli," Pauline murmured. "Take *me* home tonight, and let *her* find another way."

Eli brushed Pauline's hand aside. "I can't do that. I brought Laura to the singin', and I'll see that she gets home." He sniffed. "Besides, I love her, and just as soon as she joins the church, I'm gonna ask her to be my wife."

Pauline's face was pinched like a dried-up prune. "You're

not thinkin' straight, Eli. You haven't been right in the head since that fancy woman came sashayin' into your life."

He was about to respond, but his words were cut off when Pauline kissed him full on the mouth. It took him completely by surprise, and he wasn't sure what to do. He didn't have to think long, because Laura came sauntering up, and he could tell right away she was hopping mad.

"What's going on here?"

Pauline pivoted toward Laura. "What's it look like? Eli was kissin' me."

Eli felt his face flame. "Pauline, that just ain't so."

"I was remindin' Eli how good we are together, and he just up and kissed me," Pauline declared.

Eli could see Laura's face in the moonlight, and it was about as red as his felt. How was he ever going to make her understand the way things really happened? He knew she was a bit insecure in their relationship, and this escapade of Pauline's sure wouldn't help any.

"I should have known you were up to no good when I saw you leave the barn," Laura shouted in Pauline's face.

"Me?" Pauline countered. "All I did was talk to Eli, and he—"

Eli touched Pauline's arm, and she whirled back around to face him. "I know you're not happy 'bout me and Laura, but lyin' ain't gonna help ya none," he stated.

Pauline shrugged his hand away and stalked off. "You'll be sorry you chose her and not me. Just wait and see if you're not," she hollered over her shoulder.

Laura was fit to be tied. Did Eli really make the first move or had Pauline deliberately kissed him just to stir up trouble? Even if it broke her heart, she had to know what transpired.

"Are ya ready to go home?" Eli asked, giving her a sheepish look.

"I was ready half an hour ago," she snapped. "And don't go thinking you can soft-soap me with that cute, little boy look of yours, either."

"You remind me of *Enwiedicher Hund*," Eli said with

deep chuckle. "You've got quite a temper, but seein' how you acted when ya saw me and Pauline together let's me know how much ya love me."

Laura folded her arms and scowled at him. "I'm beginning to know more of your language, and I'll have you know, Eli Yoder, I do not look like a mad dog."

He tickled her under the chin. "You do love me, right?"

She groaned softly. "You know I do. That's why it always makes me angry whenever I see that woman with you." She leaned a bit closer to him. "Tell me the truth, Eli. Did she kiss you, or was it the other way around?"

Eli pursed his lips. "She kissed me. Honest."

"But why? Did you encourage her in any way?"

He shook his head. "She knows I love you, Laura. She's just jealous and wants to make ya think there's somethin' goin' on with us." He helped her into the buggy. "Think about it. Who's the woman I've been courtin' all summer?"

"As far as I know, only me," she replied coolly.

Eli went around and took his own seat, then picked up the reins and got the horse moving. "Let's stop by Paradise Lake on the way home. It's a *wunderbaar* night, and—"

"I don't think so, Eli," she said, flipping the ties of her head covering to the back of her neck. "I'm sure a trip to the lake would be real romantic, but to be perfectly honest, I was kind of hoping it would be me you'd be kissing tonight, not Pauline."

Eli reached over and took her hand. *"Jah,* I was wantin' that, too."

Laura sighed deeply and gazed up at the night sky. It was a beautiful evening, and the horizon was lit by hundreds of twinkling fireflies. The buggy ride should have been magical for both of them. Instead, Pauline had thrown a damper on things.

"I'm not much in the mood for love or romance now, so I think it would be good if we head straight to your sister's house," Laura said regrettably.

Eli moaned. "I'm not the least bit happy 'bout it, but, *jah*, okay. Maybe our next date'll go better."

⁂

With the exception of Eli, Laura felt closer to her future sister-in-law than she did the rest of his family. Martha Rose had patiently taught her to use the old treadle sewing machine, showed her how to bake those dreadful shoofly pies, and had given her lessons in milking, gathering eggs, and slopping the pigs. It was none of those things that made Martha Rose seem special, though. It was her friendly attitude and the way she'd accepted a complete stranger into her home. Laura wasn't sure if it was Martha Rose's hospitable nature, or if she was only doing it to please her brother. Either way, living with this young woman for the past few months had helped Laura understand the true meaning of friendship.

Having been raised as an only child, in a home where she lacked nothing, Laura knew she was spoiled. The Amish lived such a simple life, and yet they seemed happy and content with their lot. It was a mystery she couldn't explain. Even more surprising was the fact that on days like today, she almost felt one with the Plain People. Their slow-paced, quiet lifestyle held a certain measure of appeal. Although Laura still missed modern conveniences and the freedom to dress as she pleased, she also enjoyed some things about being Amish.

Little Ben Zook was one of the things she enjoyed most. He often followed her around, asking questions and pointing out things she'd never noticed before. He was doing it now, out in his mother's herb garden.

"Es gookt verderbt schee doh," the child said, pointing to a clump of mint.

Laura nodded. *"Jah,* it looks mighty nice here." She plucked off a leaf and rubbed it between her fingers, the way she'd seen Martha Rose do on several occasions. *"Appeditlich*—delicious," she said with a chuckle.

Ben sniffed deeply and smiled. *"Appeditlich!"*

Laura was amazed at his appreciation for herbs, flowers,

and all the simple things found on the farm. Most of the English children she knew needed TV, video games, and hordes of mechanical toys to keep them entertained. Was this really a better way of life? Would it be a mistake to ask Eli to become fancy?

She shook her head, as though trying to knock some sense into it. Of course she would ask him to leave someday. After all, it was ridiculous to think she could completely adjust to the Amish way of life. It would strip away her identity. If she remained Plain, she would miss out on all the good things the world had to offer. After all, she had needs, desires, and goals. Those didn't include a life of hard work or a house full of *kinder*. The truth was, in spite of Laura's fascination with little Ben, she had no desire to have children of her own. If she ever were to get pregnant, she would be fat and even dowdier than she was now. No, she could never let that happen.

❧

The baptismal ceremony and introduction of new members was scheduled for early October. Laura kept reminding herself that she needed to be ready by then, since Amish weddings were usually held in late November, after the harvest was done. If she wasn't able to join the church before then, it would be another whole year before she and Eli could be married. Of course, he hadn't actually proposed yet, but she was hopeful it would be soon.

For that matter, Eli still hadn't kissed her. She worried he might have lost interest in her. Maybe he was in love with Pauline and just wouldn't admit it. If only she could be sure. She'd given up a lot to be with him, so why didn't he show some appreciation?

Laura saw more of Eli's sister than she did him these days. His job in town at the furniture store kept him busy enough, but now he was also helping his father and brothers with the harvest. Over the last month she'd only seen him twice, and that was on biweekly church days.

"So much for courting," Laura complained as she trudged

wearily toward the chicken coop. "If I weren't so afraid of losing Eli to Pauline, I'd put my foot down and give him an ultimatum. I'd tell him either he'd better come see me at least once a week, or I'm going home to Minnesota."

There was just one problem. Laura didn't want to go home—at least not without Eli. She would endure a bit longer, but if things didn't change by the time she was baptized, she planned to have a long talk with Eli Yoder and set him straight on a few things!

❧

The big day finally arrived. This was the Sunday for baptism and church membership.

Laura was nervous as a cat about to have kittens, as she paced back and forth across the kitchen floor, waiting for Amon to pull the buggy out front.

Little Ben jerked on his mother's apron while she stood at the cupboard, packing jars of pickled beets into a cardboard box. "These will go *gut* with our Sunday lunch," she told Laura.

"Ich will mit dir," Ben whined.

"I know you wanna go," Martha Rose said. "As soon as Papa gets the buggy ready."

Ben smiled, then he reached up and touched his mother's stomach. *"Buppli."*

Laura stopped pacing and whirled around to face Martha Rose. *"Buppli?* Are you pregnant, Martha Rose?"

Martha Rose nodded. *"Jah.* I found out for sure a few days ago."

"How is it that Ben knew and I didn't?"

"He was there when I told Amon. I planned to tell you soon."

"Oh," was all Laura could manage. Maybe she wasn't as much a part of this family as she'd believed.

Amon stuck his head through the open doorway and grinned at them. A short thatch of blond hair hung across his forehead, and his brown eyes seemed so sincere. "All set?"

Martha Rose nodded. "I've got my lunch contribution packed." She smiled at Laura. "Let's be off then, for we sure wouldn't wanna be late for Laura's baptism."

❧

Eli paced nervously across the front porch of their farmhouse. Today's preaching service would be held here, and he could hardly wait. This was the day Laura would become one of them. This was the day he. . .

The sight of Amon Zook's buggy pulling into the yard halted Eli's thoughts. He skirted around a wooden bench and leaped off the porch, skipping over all four steps.

Laura offered him a tentative smile as she stepped down from the buggy. He took her hand and gave it a squeeze. "This is the day we've both been waitin' for, Laura."

She nodded, and he noticed there were tears in her eyes.

"What's wrong? You ain't havin' second thoughts, I hope."

"No, I'm just a bit nervous. What if I don't say or do the right things? What if—"

He hushed her words by placing two fingers against her lips. "You went through the six weeks of religious trainin' just fine. Today's only a formality. Say and do whatever the bishop asks. Everything will be okay, you'll see."

"I hope so," she whispered.

The service started a few minutes after Eli and Laura entered the house. He took his seat on the men's side, and she sat with the women.

The song leader led the congregation in several hymns, all sung in the usual singsong fashion, then everyone stood for Scripture reading. Next, Bishop Weaver gave the main message. When he finished, he cleared his throat a few times and said in a clear, booming voice, "Today, twenty young people have expressed their faith in Christ by requestin' baptism and membership into this church."

He motioned to the applicants, who all stood and filed to the front of the room.

Laura's legs were shaking as she knelt before the bishop.

He poured a small amount of water from a ceramic pitcher and let it drip onto her head. "Do you believe Jesus is the Son of God, and that He died for you?"

"I do," she replied. *Do you really?* a little voice niggled at the back of her mind. *Do you truly know Me as your Lord and Savior?*

Laura chose to ignore the silent reproof. She would have plenty of time to think about her relationship to God. Right now, all she wanted was to be with Eli. Her love for him was all that mattered.

eleven

The service was finally over, and Laura felt such relief as she stepped outside into the crisp fall air. It was official. She was no longer a fancy English woman. For as long as she and Eli chose to remain Amish, she would be Plain.

Most of the women were busy getting the lunch meal set out, but Laura didn't care about helping. All she wanted to do was find Eli. It didn't take her long to spot him, talking with the bishop over near the barn.

Are they talking about me? Is Eli asking Bishop Weaver if he thinks I'm sincere? Laura grabbed the porch railing and gripped it as if her very life depended on it. *What if the bishop knows I'm not a true believer? What if he's counseling Eli to break up with me?*

"We could use another pair of hands in the kitchen," Martha Rose said, as she stepped up behind Laura. "The *Mannsleit* are waitin' to eat."

Laura spun around to face her. "Why don't the *menfolk* fix the meal and wait on us women once in awhile?"

Martha Rose poked Laura's arm. "You're such a kidder. Everyone knows it's a woman's duty to serve the men."

Laura opened her mouth, fully intending to argue the subject, but something stopped her. She had just joined the Amish church. It wouldn't be good to say or do anything that might get her in trouble. Especially not with Eli out there talking to Bishop Weaver. She might be reprimanded or even shunned if she messed up now.

"What do you need help with?" Laura asked.

"Why don'tcha pour coffee for the men and milk for the boys?" Martha Rose suggested. "The pitchers are over there, on the long wooden plank we're usin' as a servin' table."

Laura shrugged and started down the porch steps. *"Jah,* okay. Whatever you say," she muttered under her breath.

જ

Lunch was over, and everyone had eaten until they were full. Laura was just finishing with the cleanup when she caught sight of Eli heading her way.

"Come with me for a walk," he whispered, taking Laura's hand and leading her away from the house.

"Where are we going?" she asked breathlessly.

"You'll see."

A few minutes later, they were standing under a huge weeping willow tree, on one side of the house, away from curious stares. Eli's fingers touched Laura's chin, tipping her head back until they were staring into each other's eyes. "You're truly one of us now," he murmured.

She nodded, feeling as though her head might explode from the anticipation of what she felt certain was coming.

Eli bent his head, and his lips touched hers in a light, feathery kiss. She moaned softly as the kiss deepened.

When Eli pulled away, she leaned into him for support, feeling as if her breath had been snatched away. It seemed as though she'd waited all her life to be kissed like that. Not a kiss of passion, the way Dean Carlson had done, but a kiss with deep emotion. Eli Yoder loved her with all his heart. She was sure of it now.

"I can finally speak the words that have been in my heart all these months," Eli said, gazing deeply into her eyes. "I love you, Laura, and I want ya to be my wife."

Tears welled up in her eyes and spilled over onto her cheeks. "Oh, Eli, I love you, too." She hugged him tightly. "Yes. . .I will marry you!"

"I just spoke with Bishop Weaver," Eli said. "At the next preachin', he's gonna tell the congregation we're officially *published.* We're to be married on the third Thursday in November."

Laura blinked away another set of tears. "I'm so happy I could dance."

His eyebrows furrowed. "The Amish don't dance, Laura."

She slapped him playfully on the arm. "I know that, silly. It was just an expression."

Eli's frown remained firmly in place. "If you're gonna be one of us, you'll need to get rid of your English expressions and learn to speak, think, and act as we do."

Laura swallowed hard. She knew his request was legitimate, but it wasn't going to be easy. It wasn't in her nature to be submissive or look plain. While she might have agreed to become Amish for a time, her ultimate goal was to marry Eli and convince him to become part of her world. She would bide her time, obey all the rules, and even try to speak and act like an Amish. Deep inside, she would always be fancy, though, and she hoped someday Eli would be as well.

Eli thought his heart would burst from the sheer joy of knowing Laura would soon be Mrs. Eli Yoder. She loved him, he was sure of it. Why else would she have thrown her old life aside and agreed to become Plain? He would never have admitted it, but *his* feet felt like dancing today. He wanted to shout to the world that he was the luckiest man alive and had found a most special woman.

While he wasn't able to shout it to the world, Eli knew he could share his news with the family. Grabbing Laura by the hand, he started to run.

"Where are we going?"

"To tell my folks our *gut* news."

Laura skidded to a halt. "Do you think that's such a good idea? I mean, can't you wait and tell them later. . .after you go home?"

Eli grimaced. "Now why would I wanna wait that long? The family deserves to hear our news now, when we're together."

"They may not want you marrying a foreigner," Laura argued. "Your mother doesn't like me, and—"

Eli stopped her words with another kiss. When he stepped back, he said softly, "You're not a foreigner anymore, Laura, and I'm sure Mom likes ya just fine."

Laura drew in a deep breath, releasing it with a moan. "Okay. Let's get this over with so we can spend some quality time together."

They found Eli's parents sitting on the porch, visiting with Martha Rose and Amon. Little Ben was playing at their feet, dragging a piece of yarn in front of the yellow barn cat's nose.

Eli led Laura up the steps and motioned her to take a seat in one of the empty chairs. He pulled out another one and sat down beside her.

"Today's baptism was *gut*," Mom said, looking over at Laura. "We welcome you into our church."

"*Jah*, you're one of us now," Pop agreed.

"Thank you, Mr. and Mrs. Yoder," Laura said, offering them a smile that seemed almost forced.

In an attempt to reassure her, Eli took her hand. "Laura has agreed to become my wife," he said, looking first at his parents, then his sister and brother-in-law. "We plan to be married in November."

Mom and Pop exchanged glances, and Eli was afraid they might say something negative about his plans. Much to his relief, Mom smiled and nodded. "We hope you'll be happy bein' Amish, Laura, and we hope you will make our son happy as well."

Pop nodded. "*Jah*, for Eli's a fine man, with much love to give. He'll make a *gut* husband and father, just you wait and see."

Martha Rose got up from her seat and bent down to give Laura a hug. "Congratulations. Soon we'll be like sisters."

Amon extended his hand to Eli and added his well wishes.

Eli grinned. "Laura was a bit nervous 'bout tellin' ya the news, but I knew you'd all share in our joy."

Laura shot him a look that could only be defined as exasperated. Maybe he'd said too much. It could be that he shouldn't have said anything about the way she was feeling.

He was trying to think up something to make her feel better, when Pop commented, "Say, Eli, if you're gonna marry this little gal, then don'tcha think you should try to fatten her up some?"

Eli looked at Laura, then back at his father. "Why would I do that, Pop?"

"Yes, why would he?" Laura echoed.

"I've seen her at mealtime, and she don't hardly eat anything," Pop contended. "Why, she'll waste away to nothin' if she don't start eatin' more."

Laura stood up quickly, nearly knocking over her chair. "I have no intention of becoming fat, Mr. Yoder!"

Pop tipped his head back and howled. "She's a feisty one, now ain't she, Son?" When he finally quit laughing, he looked at Laura and said, "If we're gonna be kinfolk, then I think you should start callin' me Johnny. Mr. Yoder makes me feel like an old man." He glanced over at Mom and gave her knee a few pats. "I'm not old yet, am I, Mary Ellen?"

Mary Ellen clicked her tongue as she pushed his hand aside. "Go on with ya, now, Johnny Yoder. You've always been a silly boy, and I guess you always will be."

Mom and Pop started howling to beat the band. Soon Martha Rose and Amon were chuckling pretty good, too.

Laura was standing there, tapping her toe against the wooden porch, and Eli figured it was time to end it all before she said or did something that would probably embarrass them both.

He stood up and grabbed her hand. "I think Laura and I should take a walk down to the creek. She needs to get cooled off, and I need to figure out how I ended up with such a laughable family."

❧

Two weeks later, Laura and Eli were to be officially *published* at the close of the preaching service. Church was held in the Zook home, so it made things easy for Laura, who, according to Amish custom, had to wait upstairs in her room until the conclusion of the service. Any other time, this arrangement would have suited her just fine, but today she was a ball of nerves and wanted to know what was going on.

She paced back and forth in front of the window. Every once in awhile she would go to the door and listen. She could hear the steady hum of Bishop Weaver's deep voice, but she couldn't quite make out his words.

Finally, after what seemed like an eternity, she heard the congregation sing their closing hymn. It was over. She could finally go downstairs and help with the meal.

In the kitchen, she found Martha Rose, Mary Ellen, Anna and Rachel Beachy, as well as their mother, Rebekah. Everyone had a job to do, even crippled Rebekah, who sat at the table in her wheelchair, buttering huge stacks of bread.

Laura offered Martha Rose a cheery smile. "Is it official? Did the bishop announce the date for our wedding?"

Martha Rose nodded and handed Laura a jar of pickled beets. "It'll be the third Thursday of November, and here's somethin' for you to do."

Laura glanced at the other four women, but they all seemed focused on their job of making ham and cheese sandwiches. She shrugged and took the jar over to the cupboard, wondering why no one seemed to care much about her upcoming marriage.

As Laura forked out beet slices and placed them on a platter, her nose wrinkled. She hated the smell of pickled beets. If she lived to be a hundred, she'd never figure out what anyone saw in those disgusting, pungent things! She had just finished putting the last one on the plate, when Pauline Hostetler entered the kitchen.

"The tables are set up, and all the other women are busy settin' out things," she said, looking at Martha Rose. "Do ya have anything ready for me to carry out?"

"You can take this plate of sandwiches." Mary Ellen held up a tray, and Pauline took it from her.

She was just about to the door, when Martha Rose spoke. "Laura, why don'tcha go with Pauline? You can take the beets, then stay to help pour beverages."

Laura drew in a deep breath and let it out in a rush. The last thing she needed was another close encounter with her rival. She didn't wish to make a scene, however, so she followed Pauline out the back door.

They had no more than stepped onto the porch, when Pauline whirled around and faced Laura. "You think you've won Eli's heart," she hissed, "but you're not married yet, so there's still some hope. You may have fooled Eli, but I can see right through ya."

Laura took a few steps back, wanting to get away from Pauline, and wondering if the young woman really did know she wasn't being completely honest with Eli. Sure, she loved him and wanted to get married. She had become Amish, too, but deep down inside, she was still Laura Meade, a fancy English woman who wanted modern things and didn't think she needed God. After all, she'd managed to get Eli, hadn't she? She'd done that all by herself. God had nothing to do with it.

"I'm sure Eli will come to his senses soon," Pauline continued. "He's blinded by romantic notions right now, but one of these days he'll realize you're not really one of us." She gazed into Laura's eyes, making her feel like a young child who'd been caught stealing pennies from a piggy bank. "I don't trust you, Laura Meade. When Eli sees the real you and casts ya aside, I'll be there, ready and willin' to become his wife."

Laura's mind whirled as she tried to think of an appropriate comeback. All she could think to do was run—far away from Pauline's piercing gaze. She practically flew down the stairs, dropped the platter of beets on the table, and sprinted off toward the creek.

❧

Eli was just rounding the corner of the house, when he caught sight of Laura running off. He was about to call out to her, but Pauline stopped him. "Let her go," she insisted. "Come sample the chocolate chip cookies I made."

Eli's forehead wrinkled. "What's goin' on, Pauline? Did you and Laura have words?"

Pauline placed the plate of sandwiches on the table and motioned him to follow her around the side of the house. When they were out of earshot and scrutinizing eyes, she stopped and placed both hands on Eli's shoulders.

He shrugged them away. "What's this all about?"

"That English woman will never make you happy. She's an outsider and she always will be. She doesn't belong here, so you'd better think twice 'bout marryin' her."

Eli felt his face flood with color. How dare Pauline speak to him that way! Who did she think she was, trying to turn him against Laura?

"I love Laura," he said through clenched teeth, "and she's not an outsider. Do I need to remind you that she joined the church and has agreed to abide by our *Ordnung?*"

Pauline shook her finger in his face. "You're the most pig-headed man I've ever met, Eli Yoder! You're blinded by her beautiful face and smooth-talkin' words, but I know what's in her heart."

"Is that so?" he shouted. "What gives ya the right to try and read someone else's mind?"

"I didn't say 'mind,' Eli. I said, 'heart.' I have a sixth sense about things, and my senses are tellin' me—"

"I don't care what your senses are sayin'," Eli interrupted. He drew in a deep breath to steady his nerves and tried to offer her a smile. "Look, Pauline, I'm sorry things didn't work out between us, but if you'll search your own heart, instead of tryin' to see what's in others', I'm sure you'll realize we could never be anything more than friends."

Pauline planted her hands on her hips, and her blue eyes flashed angrily. "We could've been more than friends, if she hadn't come along and filled your head with all sorts of fancy English ideas."

Eli was trying so hard to be civil, but he'd had just about enough of Pauline's meddling. He had to get away from her.

He needed to be with Laura.

"I never meant to hurt ya," he said sincerely, "but I love Laura with all my heart, and she loves me. She gave up bein' English so's we could be together, and nothin' you say is gonna change my mind. Is that clear enough?"

Pauline's eyes filled with tears, making Eli feel like a big heel. He really was sorry for hurting her, but it didn't change anything. He didn't love her now and never had. Even when they'd been courting, he'd only seen her as a friend.

Eli gently touched her arm. "I pray you'll find someone else to love." He walked away quickly, hoping she wouldn't follow. His life was with Laura, and she needed him now.

੨੨

Laura leaned heavily against the trunk of a tree as she gazed at the bubbling creek. *Maybe I made a mistake thinking I could become part of a world so plain and simple. Maybe Pauline is right and Eli does belong with her.*

She sucked in her bottom lip, and a fresh set of tears coursed down her cheeks. Could Pauline really see through her? Did the accusing young woman know Laura was only pretending to have changed?

How could she? Laura reasoned. *No one knows what's in my heart or mind. I've taken my biblical training classes, studied the Amish language, and learned how to cook, sew, and keep house. I wear plain clothes and no makeup, and I'm living without electricity or any other modern conveniences. What more is there? Why would Pauline think I'm not to be trusted?*

Because you're not, a little voice reminded. *You're lying to Eli, and you're lying to yourself.*

Laura dropped to the ground and sobbed. She *was* lying to Eli, but to herself? She knew exactly what she wanted out of life. A big, beautiful home, lots of money, and Eli Yoder. She wanted him more than anything. If she had to lie a little in order to make him think she really had become Amish, what harm had been done? It would only be until after the wedding. Then she could tell him how unhappy the Plain life made her and beg him to become English.

Laura jerked her head when someone touched her shoulder. She looked up and saw the face of the man she loved staring down at her.

"What's wrong? Why are ya cryin?" he asked, helping Laura to her feet.

"I–I had a little encounter with your ex-girlfriend," she said, sniffing and reaching up to wipe the tears from her face. "Pauline hates me, and she's gonna try to come between us."

"No, she's not," he said firmly. "I just spoke with Pauline, and I put her in her place, but good."

"You did?"

He pulled her into his arms. "I told Pauline it's you I love, and nothin' she says will ever change my mind."

"You mean it?"

"*Jah,* I do. Pauline and I have never been anything more'n friends, and she knows it. I don't know why she's bent on makin' trouble, but don't you worry, 'cause I'll never stop lovin' ya, Laura." Eli bent to kiss her, and Laura felt like she was drowning in his love. Everything would be all right. Things were working according to plan, and soon she'd have all she'd ever wanted.

twelve

Laura was excited about the wedding and had been given permission for her parents to attend. The bishop made it clear he wanted no other English invited to the solemn occasion, so this meant neither Shannon nor Darla could come.

Leaving Darla out didn't really bother Laura, since her school chum probably would not find much enjoyment being around "farmers." Besides, the last letter she'd gotten from Darla said she'd finished school and was working in Philadelphia, doing window designing for one of the big department stores. Darla would no doubt be working on the day of Laura's wedding.

Laura did feel bad about not inviting Shannon, though. They'd been best friends since they were kids, and each had promised the other they'd someday be in one another's weddings.

Laura decided to ask Eli's sister to be her main attendant, and her other two attendants were going to be Martha Rose's friends, Anna Beachy and Nancy Frey, the schoolteacher. The ceremony would be held at Amon and Martha Rose's house, since Laura was still living with them.

With only a few weeks until the wedding, there was much to be done. Martha Rose helped Laura sew a simple wedding dress, and they spent many hours baking and cleaning house. Several ladies in the community offered their help, and a few men volunteered to set up tables, benches, and move furniture out of the way.

"When are your parents arrivin'?" Martha Rose asked Laura as the two of them scrubbed the kitchen floor.

"Day before the wedding," Laura answered, swiping the back of her hand across her damp forehead.

"They're more than welcome to stay here. We have plenty of room," Martha Rose said.

Laura nodded. "I know you do, and it's a very kind offer, but Mom and Dad are hotel kind of people. I don't think they'd last five minutes without TV or a microwave."

Martha Rose pursed her lips. "You're managin'."

That's because I have a purpose. I won't always be stuck looking like a frump or wearing my nails down to a nubbin. Laura feigned a smile. "I'm learning."

❧

Laura and Martha Rose were seated at the kitchen table, with little Ben playing on the floor nearby. Martha Rose was mending a pair of Amon's trousers, and Laura was hemming her wedding dress. "My folks should be here soon," she remarked.

"You said they were flyin' in and would be rentin' a car to drive out?" Martha Rose asked.

Laura nodded. "I wanted them to meet all of you before the wedding, so tomorrow won't be too much of a shock."

Martha Rose frowned. "Why would they be shocked?"

"The Amish lifestyle is a bit different from what they're used to." Laura sighed deeply. "I just hope they don't try to talk me out of marrying Eli."

"Why would they do that? I'm sure you've told 'em how much you love my brother."

"Oh, yes, and Dad said if I was happy, then he was, too." Laura grinned. "I think it gives him pleasure to see me get what I want."

"Havin' one's way is not always of the Lord, Laura," Martha Rose admonished. "We're taught to be selfless, not self-centered. Surely you learned that from your religious trainin' prior to baptism."

"Yes, yes, of course," Laura stammered. "I just meant, when I was younger and didn't know much about religious things, I was rather spoiled." She chuckled. "Dad still thinks of me as his little girl, but I know he and Mom want my happiness."

"So, you're happy bein' Amish?"

"Of course. Why wouldn't I be?"

Their conversation was interrupted when a car came up the graveled driveway, causing the two farm dogs to carry on.

Laura jumped up and darted to the back door. "It's them! My folks are here!" She jerked the door open and ran down the steps.

Her father was the first to step from the car, and the bundle of fur in his hands brought a squeal of delight from Laura's lips. "Foosie!" Her arms went around Dad's waist, and she gave him a big hug.

"Your mother and I thought you might like your cat, now that you're about to be married and will soon have your own home."

Mom stepped out of the car and embraced Laura. "It's so good to see you." She frowned and took a few steps back. "Oh, dear, you've changed! What happened to our beautiful, vibrant daughter? What have these Plain People done to you?"

Laura had expected some reservation on her parents' part, but her mother's rude comment took her by surprise. If she wasn't beautiful anymore, did that mean she was ugly?

"Laura is still beautiful. . .in a plain sort of way," Dad said, handing the cat to Laura.

Laura rubbed her nose against Foosie's soft fur and sniffed deeply. At least someone still loved her. She could feel tears stinging the back of her eyes. "I–I don't think I can keep Foosie."

"Why not?" Mom asked.

"Eli and I will be living with his parents until their addition is complete," Laura explained. "They might not appreciate having an inside cat underfoot."

"That's nonsense!" Dad exclaimed. "I thought the Amish liked animals." He gazed around the farmyard, until he spotted the cows in the field. "See, there's a bunch of animals."

"And don't forget those dreadful dogs that barked at us when we pulled in," Mom added.

"Those are farm animals," Laura reminded. "They're not pampered pets."

"Be that as it may, I would think your husband would want you to be happy," Mom said.

Before Laura could respond, Martha Rose was at her side. "I'm Martha Rose Zook." She extended her hand toward Laura's mother.

Mom smiled and shook the offered hand, and Dad stepped forward to greet Martha Rose. "I'm Wesley Meade, and this is my wife, Irene."

"I'm glad to meet ya."

"Nice place you've got here. I always did have a hankering for the country life," Dad said, sounding a bit wistful.

"Won'tcha please come inside? It's kinda nippy out, and I've got plenty of hot coffee and some freshly baked brownies waitin'," Martha Rose offered.

"Sounds good to me," Dad replied enthusiastically.

Everyone followed Martha Rose to the house. When they stepped onto the back porch, Laura stopped. "Uh, what would you like me to do with my cat?"

Martha Rose blinked. *"Ach,* my! I didn't realize you were holdin' a cat. Where'd it come from?"

"We brought it from Minnesota," Dad answered. "Foosie is Laura's house pet."

Laura rocked back and forth on her heels. What if Martha Rose made her throw Foosie out in the barn? She knew the cat would never get along with farm cats. Besides, she might get fleas!

"Bring the cat inside," Martha Rose said, opening the door. "I'm sure Ben would love to play with her awhile."

Once her folks were seated at the kitchen table, Laura placed Foosie on the floor beside Ben. He squealed with delight and hugged the cat around the neck.

"Now don't *knutsche* too hard," Martha Rose admonished her son. She quickly poured mugs of steaming coffee, and Laura passed around a plate of brownies.

"What's a *knutsche?*" Mom asked.

"It means 'cuddle,' " Laura explained.

"Schnuck! Schnuck!" Ben hollered as Foosie licked the end of his nose.

"Ben thinks Foosie is cute," Laura said, before either of her parents could raise the question.

"Laura says you plan on stayin' at a hotel in Lancaster while you're here," Martha Rose said as she handed Dad a mug.

He nodded. "That's right. We made our reservations as soon as Laura phoned and told us about the wedding."

"You're welcome to stay here."

Mom smiled sweetly. "That's kind of you, Martha Rose, but I think it would be less hectic if we stay at the hotel."

Martha Rose shrugged. "Whatever ya think best."

"I made my own wedding dress," Laura said, holding up the pale blue dress she'd been hemming earlier.

Mom frowned. "Oh, my! It doesn't look anything like a traditional wedding gown."

"It's a traditional Amish dress," Martha Rose stated.

Mom shrugged. "I see."

Laura could see by the look on her mother's face that she was anything but happy about this plain wedding. For that matter, she was probably upset about Laura marrying an Amish man. Mom most likely thought her only daughter had completely lost her mind. However, she had no idea Laura was planning to marry Eli, gain his trust, then ask him to leave the Amish faith and move back to Minnesota. If Mom had known, she might not look quite so grief-stricken.

I don't want Mom and Dad to let my secret out. So I'll tell them my plans when the time is right. Until then, they'll just have to accept what is going on. Laura turned to look at her dad. He was grinning like a Cheshire cat, and obviously enjoying the homemade brownies, for he'd already eaten three.

"Eli and his parents are coming over for supper," Laura said, changing the subject again. "I'm so anxious for you to meet him."

"Jah," Martha Rose agreed. "Eli's right excited 'bout meetin' your folks, too."

ð

The back door opened, and Eli, his brothers, and their folk entered the house. Laura rushed to his side. "My parents are here, and I'm so glad you came!"

Introductions were soon made, and everyone took seats at the table. Laura and Martha Rose served a scrumptious supper of ham, bread stuffing, mashed potatoes, green beans, chow-chow, and homemade bread.

All heads bowed in silent prayer, and Laura was relieved when her parents followed suit. Even though they only went to church at Christmas and Easter, they did know social graces.

"Laura tells me you work in a law office," Eli said as he passed Laura's dad the platter of ham.

"Sure do. In fact, I have several other lawyers working for me." Dad grinned and forked two huge pieces of meat onto his plate. "Umm. . .this sure looks tasty."

"Pop raises hogs," Lewis spoke up. "He's always got plenty of meat to share with Martha Rose and Amon."

Johnny Yoder nodded and spooned himself a sizable helping of bread stuffing. "Yep, I'm not braggin' now, but I think I've got some of the finest hogs around."

Mary Ellen patted her husband's portly stomach. "*Jah,* and some pretty *gut* milkin' cows, too."

Laura moved the fork slowly around her plate, wishing this conversation would take a turn. Just talking about food made her feel fat.

As if he knew what she was thinking, Eli's father glanced over at her dad and frowned. "Wesley, how much influence do ya have on that daughter of yours?"

Dad gulped down some milk before he answered. "I'm not altogether sure. Why do you ask?"

Johnny pointed a finger at Laura. "She eats like a bird. Just look at her plate. Hardly a thing on it!"

Laura knew everyone was looking at her, and her face flooded with the heat of embarrassment. "I eat enough to sustain myself. I just don't think one needs to become chubby in order to prove one's worth."

The room became deathly quiet, and she knew she'd said too much. By Amish standards, elders were not to be argued with. . .especially not the parents of your betrothed.

"I—um—meant to say, I prefer to watch my weight," she quickly amended. "If others choose to overeat, that's their right." *Not much better,* she realized a little too late.

"Laura, what are ya sayin'?" Eli whispered. "Are ya tryin' to make some kinda trouble tonight?"

She shook her head. "I'm sorry. I don't know what came over me."

Tonight was supposed to be a happy occasion. . .a time for Laura's folks to get to know Eli and his family. Things had been going so well, but now there was tension, and she was the cause. Would she ever learn to keep her big mouth shut?

"I think our daughter might be a bit nervous," Laura's mother said, offering one of her most pleasant smiles. "It isn't every day she introduces her father and I to her future husband and in-laws, you know."

Martha Rose nodded. "I think you could be right, Irene. Laura's been jittery as a dragonfly all day. Haven't ya, Laura?"

Laura shrugged. "I suppose."

"In fact, Laura did most of the work today, just to keep her hands busy," Martha Rose added.

"I did work pretty hard, but that's because I wanted Martha Rose to rest." Laura glanced at her mother. "Martha Rose is in a family way."

Mom's eyebrows furrowed. "Family way?"

"She's pregnant, Hon," Dad said with a chuckle. "I haven't heard that expression since I was a boy growing up on the farm, but I sure can remember what 'being in a family way' means."

"Your folks were farmers?" The question came from Johnny, who leaned his elbows on the table as he scrutinized Laura's dad.

"My parents farmed a huge spread out in Montana," her

father answered. "Dad sold the farm several years ago, since none of us boys wanted to follow in his footsteps." His forehead wrinkled. "Sometimes I wonder if I made the wrong choice, becoming a fancy city lawyer instead of an old cowhand."

Little Ben, who up until this moment had been busy playing with the bread stuffing on his plate, spoke up for the first time. *"Meislin!"* he shouted, pointing to the floor and disrupting the conversation.

"Meislin? Where?" Martha Rose screeched. She was immediately on her feet.

"Schpring, bussli!" Ben hollered as he bounced up and down in his chair.

"What on earth is going on?" Laura's mother asked with a note of concern.

"Aw, it's just a few little mice, and Ben's tellin' the kitty to run," Jonas said with a deep chuckle. "That fluffy white cat will take 'em in a hurry, too, I'll bet."

"Fluffy white cat?" Mary Ellen's eyes were wide. "When did ya get an indoor cat, Martha Rose?"

Martha Rose had a broom in her hand and was running around the kitchen, swinging it this way and that. If Laura hadn't been so concerned about Foosie, she might have thought the whole scene was rather funny.

Foosie was busy dodging the broom and leaping into the air as two tiny, gray field mice scooted across the floor at lightning speed. Everyone at the table was either laughing or shouting orders at Martha Rose.

"Open the door!" Amon hollered. "Maybe they'll run outside."

"No, don't touch that door!" Laura shrieked. "Foosie might get out, and I'd never be able to catch her once the dogs discovered she was on the loose."

Foosie was almost on top of one mouse, but just as her paw came down, the critter darted for a hole under the cupboard. The other mouse followed, leaving a very confused cat sitting in front of the hole, meowing for all she was worth.

Laura's dad was laughing so hard, he had tears rolling down his cheeks. "Well, if that doesn't beat all. In all the years we've had that cat, I don't believe I've ever seen her move so fast." He wiped his eyes with a napkin and started howling again.

Laura stood up. "I don't see what's so funny, Dad. Poor Foosie has never seen a mouse before. She could have had a heart attack, tearing around the room like that."

Another round of laughter filled the room. Even Martha Rose, who only moments ago had been chasing the mice with her broom, was back in her seat, holding her sides and chuckling as hard as everyone else.

Laura just shook her head. Was all this silliness a good sign, or did it merely mean Eli's family and her parents had taken leave of their senses?

Eli reached for Laura's hand. "I think you were nervous for nothin'," he whispered in her ear. "The cat and mice game sure enough got everyone in a happy kinda mood. *Wass Got tuht ist wohl getahn*—what God doeth is well done."

❧

"Today's the big day," Martha Rose said when Laura entered the kitchen bright and early the next morning. "Did ya sleep well?"

Laura yawned and reached for a mug to pour herself some coffee. "Actually, I hardly slept a wink. I was too nervous about today."

Martha Rose pulled out a chair and motioned for Laura to take a seat. "I understand how ya feel. I was a ball of nerves on my weddin' day."

"Really? You mean, it's not just me?"

Martha Rose got another chair and seated herself beside Laura. She touched her outstretched arm. "I think all brides feel the same. Even though we love our grooms like everything, we're still kinda jittery 'bout tyin' the knot."

Laura took a long, slow drink from her cup. "I hope I can make Eli happy."

"You will. Ya love him, don'tcha?"

"Of course, but—"

"Just do your best to please him. Always trust God to help ya, and your marriage will go fine."

Laura nodded, but she wasn't sure it would be as easy as Martha Rose made it seem. Especially since she didn't have any idea how she was going to put her trust in God.

ॐ

The wedding began at nine o'clock sharp. Laura and her three attendants sat on one bench, directly in front of Bishop Weaver. On the bench across from them sat Eli and his two brothers, along with a friend, Dan, his other attendant. Laura's mother and Eli's mom sat behind Laura, and behind Eli sat his dad, Laura's father, and Amon, holding little Ben on his lap. All the other wedding guests filled the rest of the benches, making a total of 150 in attendance.

Laura, wearing her light blue, full-skirted dress, covered with a white organdy apron, sat rigid on her backless bench. *Am I really doing the right thing? Will I ever be able to convince Eli to leave the Amish faith? And if he refuses, can I possibly spend the rest of my life as a Plain woman?*

Laura knew divorce was not an option among the Amish, so no matter what Eli decided about going English, she would have to accept it and be willing to live with his decision. She glanced over at her groom, sitting straight and tall, and looking so happy. He was awfully handsome, dressed in a pair of black trousers, a matching vest, and a collarless, dark jacket. Accentuating his white cotton shirt was a black bow tie, making Eli look every bit as distinguished as any of the lawyers who worked for her father's law firm.

Bishop Weaver's booming voice drew Laura out of her musings. He was asking the wedding party to follow him and two church deacons to another part of the house. They were led upstairs and down the long hall. When they came to Laura's bedroom, the bishop opened the door. Signaling the bride and groom's attendants to wait outside, he ushered

Laura and Eli inside.

As they sat in two straight-backed chairs, the bride and groom were given instructions on the responsibilities and obligations related to marriage. Each of the deacons said a few words, quoting Scripture and admonishing the young couple to remain faithful to one another.

Half an hour later, they returned to the living room, where the congregation was singing a traditional Amish hymn. When the singing ended, one of the deacons delivered a lengthy sermon, alluding to more Bible verses related to marriage.

Laura was beginning to feel a headache coming on. She was getting mighty tired of hearing how a wife should behave. . . faithful, loving, obedient, always looking to her husband's needs. What about her needs? Didn't they matter at all?

When the sermon was over, Bishop Weaver stepped forward and motioned Eli and Laura to join him at the front of the room. Laura felt the touch of Eli's hand, and she squeezed his fingers in response. This was it. This was the moment they'd been waiting for.

There was no exchange of rings, like in most English weddings, but there were vows. "Vows not to be taken lightly," the bishop said. "Vows to be kept, for better or worse, for rich or poor, in sickness and health, 'til death do you part."

Feeling much like a toy robot, Laura repeated her vows and listened as Eli did the same. His eyes were brimming with tears, and he wore a smile that stretched from ear to ear. Eli Yoder really did love her. Now all he had to do was prove it.

thirteen

Eli and Laura moved outside to the front lawn. Even though there was a chill in the air, the sun was shining and the sky was clear blue. It was a perfect day for a wedding, and Eli was content in the knowledge that Laura Meade was now Mrs. Eli Yoder.

A reception line was formed, with those in attendance coming by to offer Eli and Laura their congratulations. When Wesley and Irene Meade hugged their daughter, they both had tears in their eyes. For one brief moment, Eli felt a pang of guilt. He knew he was the cause of Laura leaving her fancy life and becoming one of the Plain People. Because of her love for him, she wouldn't see much of her family, and she'd given up all the modern things her rich father could offer.

Eli shook hands with Laura's parents and said, "I'll take *gut* care of your daughter. I hope ya know that."

Wesley nodded. "I believe you're an honest man, Eli, and I can tell by the look on your face how much you love Laura."

"Please, let her keep Foosie," Irene put in. "She needs a touch from home."

Eli grinned. *"Jah,* I'll speak to Mom and Pop 'bout the cat. I'm sure they won't mind havin' a pet inside, just as long as it's housebroke."

"Oh, she is," Laura asserted. "Foosie's never made a mess in the house. Not even when she was a kitten."

Mom and Martha Rose came through the line next. They hugged Eli and Laura, then excused themselves to go help in the kitchen. Pop, Amon, and little Ben followed, with both men shaking Eli's hand and welcoming Laura into the family with a hug and a kiss on the cheek. Not to be outdone, Ben insisted on kissing the bride, too. In fact, it was all Amon could do to tear his son out of Laura's arms and send him off to play. It was obvious the child was enamored with Laura, and she seemed to like him equally well.

She'll make a gut *mother,* Eli mused. *Lord willin', maybe we'll have a whole house full of* kinder.

❧

The wedding meal was a veritable feast. Long tables had been set up in the living room, dining room, parlor, and for hardier individuals, some were placed outside on the lawn. Several Amish women served up platters of fried chicken, baked ham, bread filling, mashed potatoes, a variety of cooked vegetables, plenty of chow-chow, and a fine array of cookies, pies, and cakes. There was also coffee, milk, and homemade root beer.

Laura and Eli sat at their corner table, along with their attendants. There was plenty of joke-telling and friendly banter going on, and Laura was thoroughly enjoying herself.

"Eat hearty, *Frau,*" Eli said, needling Laura in the ribs with his elbow. "Today's our weddin' day, and this is no time to diet."

She leaned closer to him and smiled. "I might splurge and try a little bit of everything, but tomorrow's another day. I'll probably have five pounds to shed after this feast!"

Laura glanced across the room and saw her parents sitting at a table with Eli's folks. They seemed to be having a good time, despite the fact they hardly knew anyone.

Pauline Hostetler was among the women acting as servers. Laura didn't expect to see her at all today, much less helping out. For one brief moment, she felt pity for Pauline. She'd lost Eli to a fancy English woman, and now her heart was obviously broken.

"Wanna sneak away with me?" Eli's tender words, and the wiggling of his eyebrows, drew Laura out of her contemplations.

"Sneak away? As in leave this place?" she asked, offering him a smile.

Eli reached for her hand. "I think it's time for my bride and me to get some fresh air," he announced to those at their table. "I hope you'll excuse us."

"I'll race you to the creek," Laura said as soon as they were outside.

"You're on!" Eli shouted, then took off on a run.

Laura was breathless by the time she reached the water, and she didn't get there much behind Eli. They collapsed on the grass, ignoring the chill and laughing and tickling each other until Laura finally called a truce.

"So, it's peace you're wantin', huh?" Eli teased. "All right, but you'll have to pay a small price for it."

Laura squirmed beneath his big hands. "Oh, yeah? What kind of payment must I offer the likes of you, Eli Yoder?"

"This," he murmured against her ear. "And this." He nuzzled her neck with his cold nose. "Also this." His lips trailed a brigade of soft kisses along her chin, up her cheek, and finally they came to rest on her lips. As the kiss deepened, Laura moaned softly and snuggled closer to Eli.

When they finally pulled away, she gazed deeply into his dazzling blue eyes. "I love you, Husband, and I always will."

"And I love you, my *seelich*—blessed gift."

જ

Laura and Eli spent their first night as husband and wife at Martha Rose and Amon's house. Tomorrow they would be moving to Eli's parents' and sharing their home until the addition was built. This smaller home, added onto the main house, was where Johnny, Mary Ellen, and their two younger sons would live. Laura and Eli would remain in the larger home, since they were a new family. The building wouldn't begin until spring, and this caused Laura some concern. What would it be like living under the same roof with her in-laws? Would Mary Ellen scrutinize her every move? Would she be expected to do even more work than she had while living at the Zooks'?

Forcing her anxiety aside, Laura stepped into the kitchen. Eli had already gone to work at his job in town, and she knew her folks would be here soon to say good-bye.

Martha Rose was busy baking bread, but she looked up and

smiled when Laura entered the room. "How's the *Hochzeit?* Did ya sleep well?"

Laura shuffled across the kitchen, still feeling the effects of sleep. She nodded and yawned. "The newlyweds are fine, and I'm sorry I overslept. Eli left for work without waking me."

"Guess he thought ya needed to rest. Yesterday was a pretty big day," Martha Rose reminded.

Laura reached for the pot of coffee on the back of the wood-burning stove.

"There's still some scrambled eggs left in the warmin' oven," Martha Rose said, gesturing with her head. "Help yourself."

Laura moaned. "After all I ate yesterday, I don't think I need any breakfast."

"Oh, but breakfast is the most important meal of the day," Martha Rose argued. "And now that you're a married woman, you'll be needin' to keep up your strength."

Laura dropped into a chair at the table. "What's that supposed to mean?"

"Just that you'll soon be busy settin' up your own house."

"Not really. Eli and I will be living with your folks, remember?"

Martha Rose nodded. *"Jah,* but not for long. If I know my brother, he'll be workin' long hours on that addition." She winked at Laura. "He's a man in love, and I think he'd kinda like to have ya all to himself."

Laura felt the heat of a blush stain her face. "I–I'd like that, too," she admitted.

"So, dish up some eggs, and while you're at it, why not have some of that leftover apple pie from the weddin'?"

Laura opened her mouth to offer a rebuttal, but the sound of a car pulling into the yard drew her to the window instead. "It's my parents. They've come to say good-bye." She jerked open the door and ran down the stairs. If she were going to get all teary-eyed, she'd rather not do it in front of Eli's sister.

As soon as Mom and Dad stepped from the car, the three of them shared a group hug.

"I'll miss you," Laura said tearfully.

"Be happy," her mother whimpered.

"If you ever need anything. . .anything at all, please don't hesitate to call," Dad said. He grinned at her. "I know you Amish don't have phones in your houses, but I hear tell it's acceptable for you to use a pay phone."

Laura nodded. "That's true, but some Amish have phones outside. Mostly those who have a home business."

"We should really go inside and say good-bye to your new sister-in-law," Mom said as she started for the house.

Laura reached out to stop her. "Martha Rose is kind of busy this morning. She said to tell you good-bye." *Why did I lie about that? Why don't I want Mom and Dad to come inside?*

Dad broke into her thoughts before she could come up with any kind of reasonable answer. "Where's Eli? We do get to tell our son-in-law good-bye, I hope."

"Eli works at a furniture store in Lancaster," Laura explained. "He left early this morning."

Mom's mouth dropped open. "The day after your wedding? Why, I've never heard of such a thing! The two of you should be on a honeymoon at some resort, not him working, and you stuck on this dreary old farm."

Laura hung her head. How could she argue with that? Especially when she'd been thinking the same thing.

Dad slipped his arm around her waist. "The Amish have some pretty strange ways, but this man you've married is a rare one. He's a hard worker, and I'm convinced he loves you."

A few tears slipped under Laura's lashes and dribbled down her cheeks. She sniffed deeply. "I love him, too, Dad, but someday I'm hoping—"

Laura's words were halted by a piercing scream. At least she thought it was a scream. She turned toward the sound coming from the front porch. Foosie was clinging to one of the support beams, and Amon's dogs were below, yapping and jumping up and down. Poor Foosie was hissing and screeching for all she was worth.

"Oh, no," Laura moaned. "Foosie must have slipped out the door behind me." She turned back to face her parents. "I'd better go rescue her, and you two had better get to the airport. You don't want to be late for your flight."

Mom gave Laura a quick peck on the cheek, then climbed into the rental car. Dad embraced Laura one final time, and just before he took his seat on the driver's side, he said, "Don't forget. . .call if you need us."

Laura nodded and blinked back tears. She offered one final wave, then raced toward the house. Even if she couldn't fix her own problems today, she could at least save her cat!

❧

Laura had visited Eli's parents' home several times, but she'd never had occasion to use the rest room. It wasn't until she and Eli moved her things to his house and were settled into their own room that Laura was hit with a sickening reality. Johnny Yoder had never installed indoor plumbing! Most of the Amish farms in the valley had indoor bathrooms, but the Yoders still used an outhouse.

When Laura expressed her dislike of the smelly facilities, Eli promised as soon as the addition was done, he would see about turning one of the upstairs closets into a bathroom.

"How am I supposed to bathe?" Laura wailed as she paced back and forth in front of their bedroom window.

"We have a galvanized tub for that," Eli answered from his seat on the bed. "You'll heat water on the stove, and—"

"And nothing!" Laura shouted. "Eli Yoder, I can hardly believe you would expect me to live under such barbaric conditions!"

Eli looked at her like she'd taken leave of her senses. "Calm down. You'll wake up the whole house, shoutin' that-away." He joined her at the window. "You've gotten used to livin' without other modern things, so I'd think you could manage this little inconvenience. After all, it's really not such a *greislich*."

She squinted her eyes at him. "It's a terrible thing to me, Eli.

And this is not a 'little' inconvenience. It's a major catastrophe!"

He clicked his tongue. "Such big words you're usin', and such resentment I see on your face." He brushed her cheek lightly with his thumb. "You've done so well adjustin' to bein' Amish, and I'm right proud of you."

How could she stay mad with him looking at her that way? His enchanting eyes were shining like the moonlight, and his chin dimple was pronounced by his charming smile.

She leaned against his chest and sighed deeply. "Promise me you'll build us a decent bathroom as soon as you can?"

"*Jah,* I promise."

⁂

The next few weeks flew by, as Laura settled into her in-laws' home during weekdays and she and Eli honeymooned at various relative and friends' homes every weekend. There wasn't much privacy for the newlyweds, and Laura always felt obligated to help out wherever they stayed. At least they were sent home with a gift from their hosts every Sunday evening. They'd already received some bedding, several jars of home-canned fruit, and a huge sack of root vegetables. Laura's favorite gift was an oval braided rug in rich autumn hues. This she placed on the bare, wooden floor in their bedroom. The room they shared had been Eli's, and as she spread it near her side of the bed, he informed her that he'd never seen the need for a rug before.

"Look how well it goes with the quilt I purchased at the farmers' market last fall," she said, motioning toward the lovely covering at the foot of their bed. "It can be the focal point of our room."

Eli raised his eyebrows. "Don't know nothin' about *focal* points in the room, but it does looks right *gut.*" He pulled Laura to his chest and rubbed his face against her cheek. "Almost as *gut* as my beautiful wife."

"Eli, you're hurting me," she complained. "Your face is so scratchy!"

He stepped back, holding her at arm's length. "It'll be better once my beard grows fully."

She thrust out her chin. "I don't see why you can't shave anymore. I think it's a silly rule that married Amish men have to wear a beard."

Eli scowled at her. "You knew it was a rule before you agreed to marry me. I don't see why you're makin' such a fuss over it now."

Laura shrugged and turned away. "Forget it. There's nothing I can do about it anyway." *At least, not now.*

❧

"I hear your sister's in a family way," Maude Hostetler said to Eli as he and Laura sat at the Hostetlers' kitchen table during one of their "visiting" weekends.

Eli grinned. "That's right, she is."

Maude glanced at Laura, sitting beside Eli. "How many *kinder* are you hopin' to have?"

Laura's face flamed, and she looked over at Eli. "As many as the good Lord allows," he replied.

Laura's expression turned from embarrassment to shock. Her mouth opened, but the only word that came out was, "Huh?"

Eli squeezed her hand under the table. "I like *kinder*. . .you like *kinder*. . .we'll have a whole house full!"

Pauline, who had been silent until now, spoke up. "I think Laura will be a great *mamm*. Can't ya just see her chubby little body runnin' around chasin' *kinder* all day?"

Everyone at the table stared at Pauline. She didn't seem to care, for she laughed and went right on with her tirade. "Before long, Laura will look like an *alte Kuh*—old cow, instead of all prim and proper, tryin' to keep her fancy ways without no one noticin'."

Matt Hostetler's fist came down hard against the table, and everyone jumped. "That'll be enough, Daughter! What's gotten into you?"

Pauline wrinkled her nose and leveled her gaze at Laura. "Why don'tcha ask *her?*"

Laura scooted her chair back and stood up. "I think we

should go, Eli. It's obvious we're not wanted here."

"That just ain't so," Maude insisted. "It's only our daughter who's bein' rude, and if she was a few years younger, she'd be taken out back to the woodshed and given a sound *bletching*. I think her bein' the baby of the family and the last one to leave the nest might've made her a bit spoiled."

Ignoring her mother's comment, Pauline pointed at Laura. "You stay and finish your supper. I'll leave!" With that, she jumped up and marched out of the room.

Eli grasped Laura's hand and pulled her gently back to her seat. "We won't be spendin' the night, but I think we should finish eatin' before we head for home."

Maude nodded. "And don't forget your weddin' gift. Matt made you a straw broom, and I have several jars of home-canned pickled beets."

Eli felt a sense of relief when Laura picked up her fork and began to eat the potpie on her plate. He knew it had been a mistake coming here, but what else was he to do? After all, the Hostetlers *had* extended an invitation.

On the buggy ride home, Eli kept glancing at Laura, slouched in her seat with her eyes closed. Truth be told, he was worried sick about his new bride. She hadn't been acting right ever since they moved in with Mom and Pop. Was it the folks she was having trouble with, or did Laura resent *him?* He had to know what was wrong, and he had to know soon.

Laura kept her eyes shut, hoping Eli would think she was asleep and wouldn't try to make conversation. The last thing she wanted was another argument, and she was pretty sure they would quarrel if she told him all the things on her mind.

As they pulled into the Yoders' driveway, Laura opened her eyes. She sat up with a start when Eli pulled the buggy over, just as he'd done many times before when he thought they needed to work things out.

"What are you doing?"

"I'm stoppin' here so we can talk."

"There's nothing to talk about."

"I think there is," he replied stiffly.

She drew in a deep breath and released it with a shudder. "What do you think we need to talk about?"

"This business between you and Pauline for one thing," he said. "How come there's so much hostility still goin' on?"

Laura groaned. "Eli, Eli, are you really so blind? Pauline's still in love with you, and she's angry with me for taking you away from her."

Eli scrunched up his nose. "If I've told ya once, I've told ya a hundred times. . .Pauline and I were never more than friends."

"She wanted it to be more," Laura argued. She balled her hands into fists. "I think your mother did, too."

"Mom?"

Laura shook her head. "Oh, Eli, don't look so wide-eyed and innocent. We've been living with your folks several weeks now. Surely you can feel the tension between me and your mother."

He merely shrugged in response.

"She's mentioned Pauline a few times, too. I think she believes Pauline would have made you a better wife."

Even in the darkened buggy, Laura could see a vein on the side of Eli's neck begin to bulge. It often did that whenever he was upset.

"Your mom is always criticizing me," Laura continued. "I can never do anything right where she's concerned."

Eli pursed his lips. "I don't believe that."

"Are you calling me a liar?"

"No, but I think I know Mom pretty well."

"You don't know her as well as you think!" Laura shouted. "She scrutinizes my work, and she—"

Eli shook his finger in front of her face. "Enough! I don't want to hear another word against my mom!"

fourteen

Christmas was fast approaching, and Laura looked on it with dread. Nothing seemed to be going right these days. She and Eli argued all the time, Foosie was an irritant to Eli's mother, Laura detested the extra chores she was expected to do, and worst of all, she hated that smelly outhouse! She was on her way there now and none too happy about it.

On previous trips to the privy, she'd encountered icky spiders, a yellow jackets' nest, and a couple of field mice. She was a city girl and hated bugs. She shouldn't have to be subjected to this kind of torture.

Laura opened the wooden door and held it with one hand as she lifted her kerosene lantern and peered cautiously inside. Nothing lurking on the floor. She held the lamp higher and was just about to step inside when the shaft of light fell on something. It was dark and furry—and it was sitting over the hole!

Laura let out a piercing scream and slammed the door. She sprinted toward the house and ran straight into Eli, coming from the barn.

"Laura, what's wrong? I heard ya hollerin' and thought one of Pop's pigs had gotten loose again."

Laura clung to Eli's jacket. "It's the outhouse. . .there's some kind of monstrous animal in there!"

Eli grinned at her. "*Kumme*—come now, it was probably just a little old mouse."

"It wasn't," she sobbed. "It was dark and furry. . .and huge!"

Eli slipped his hand in the crook of her arm. "Let's go have a look-see."

"I'm not going in there."

He chuckled. "You don't have to. I'll do the checkin'."

Laura held her breath as Eli entered the outhouse. "Be careful."

She heard a thud, followed by a loud whoop. Suddenly, the door flew open and Eli bolted out of the privy, chased by the hairy creature Laura had seen a few moments ago. It was a comical sight, but she was too frightened to see the full humor in it.

"What was that?" she asked Eli, as the two of them stood watching the critter dash into the field.

"I think it was a hedgehog," Eli said breathlessly. "The crazy thing tried to attack me, but I kicked him with the toe of my boot. . .right before I walked out of the outhouse."

Laura giggled. "Don't you mean, 'ran out of the outhouse'?"

Eli's face turned pink and he chuckled. *"Jah,* I guess I was movin' pretty fast."

The two of them stood there a few seconds, gazing into each other's eyes. Then they both started giggling. They laughed so hard, they had tears streaming down their faces, and Laura had to set the lantern on the ground for fear it would fall out of her hand. It felt good to laugh. It was something neither of them did much anymore.

When they finally got control of their emotions, Eli reached for her hand. "I'll see about indoor plumbing as soon as spring comes. I promise."

❧

Christmas morning dawned with a blanket of pristine snow covering the ground and every tree in the Yoders' yard. It looked like a picture postcard, and despite the fact that Laura missed her parents, she felt happier today than she had in weeks.

She let the dark shade fall away from the living room window and took a seat in the wooden rocker by the fireplace. Even though there was no Christmas tree or twinkle lights on the house, there were a few candles spaced around the room, along with several Christmas cards from family and friends.

Guess I did end up with an Early American look, she mused.
It's just a little plainer than I had wanted.

Laura spotted the Christmas card they'd received from her
parents, along with a substantial check. She closed her eyes
and sighed deeply. *I thought I'd be back home by Christmas.
Oh, well. . .maybe next year.*

ॐ

Eli had been looking forward to Christmas for weeks. He'd
made Laura a special gift, and this afternoon his sister and her
family would be joining them for Mom's traditional holiday
feast.

"Life couldn't be any better," he said to the horse he was
grooming. "Maybe later we'll hitch you up to the sleigh and
I'll take my beautiful wife for a ride to Paradise Lake."

The horse whinnied as if in response, and Eli chuckled.
"You kinda like that idea, don'tcha, old boy?"

When Eli entered the house a short time later, he was holding Laura's gift under his jacket. "Where's my *Frau?*" he
asked Mom, who was scurrying around the kitchen.

She nodded toward the living room. "In there. I guess she
thinks I don't need any help gettin' dinner on."

Eli merely shrugged and left the kitchen. No point getting
Mom more riled than she already was. He found Laura sitting
in the rocking chair, gazing at the fireplace. *"En freh-licher
Grischtdaag!"*

"A Merry Christmas to you, too," she replied.

Eli bent down and kissed the top of her head. "I have somethin' for ya."

Laura jumped up. "You do? What is it?"

Eli held his jacket shut. "Guess."

She wrinkled her nose. "I have no idea. Tell me. . .please."

Eli chuckled and withdrew an ornate birdhouse, painted
blue with white trim.

"Oh, Eli, it's just like the one you showed me at Farmers
Market the day we first met."

He smiled. "And now you do have a place for it."

She accepted the gift, and tears welled up in her eyes. "Thank you so much. It's beautiful."

"Does my pretty *Frau* have anything for her hardworkin' husband?" Eli asked in a teasing tone.

Laura hung her head. "I do, but I'm afraid it's not finished."

"You made me somethin'?"

She nodded. "I've been sewing you a new shirt, but your mom's kept me so busy, I haven't had time to get it hemmed and wrapped."

Eli took the birdhouse from Laura and placed it on the small table by her chair. He pulled her toward him in a tender embrace. "It's okay, my love. You'll get the shirt finished soon, and I'll appreciate it then every bit as much as I would if you'd given it to me now."

Laura rested her head against his shoulder. "I love you, Eli. Thanks for being so understanding."

❧

Silent prayer had been said, and everyone sat around the table with expectant, hungry looks on their faces. Mary Ellen had outdone herself. Huge platters were laden with succulent roast beef and mouthwatering ham. There were bowls filled with buttery mashed potatoes, candied yams, canned green beans, and coleslaw. Sweet cucumber pickles, black olives, dilled green beans, and red beet eggs were also included in the feast, as well as buttermilk biscuits and cornmeal muffins.

Everyone ate heartily. Everyone except for little Ben and Laura. Their plates were still half full when Mary Ellen brought out three pies—two pumpkin and one mincemeat— along with a tray of chocolate donuts.

Ben squealed with delight. *"Fettkuche!"*

"No donuts until you eat everything on your plate," Martha Rose scolded.

Ben's lower lip began to quiver, and his eyes filled with tears.

"Bein' a crybaby won't help you get your way," Amon admonished.

"He's only a child," Laura put in. She pulled one of the pumpkin pies close to her and helped herself to a piece. "Surely he can have one little donut."

All eyes seemed to be focused on Laura; and Ben, who'd moments ago been fighting tears, let loose with a howl that sent Laura's cat flying into the air.

"Now look what you've gone and done," Amon said, shaking his finger in Ben's face. "You've scared that poor cat half to death."

Foosie was running around the table, meowing and swishing her tail. Laura bent down and scooped her up, but the look on Mary Ellen's face was enough to let her know that in this house, cats didn't belong at the table. She mumbled an apology and deposited Foosie back on the floor.

"You're not settin' a very good example for the boy, Laura." This reprimand came from Eli's father, who was scowling at her. "If you're not gonna eat all your food, then I don't think ya should be takin' any pie." Johnny looked pointedly at Eli then. "What do you think, Son? Should your wife be allowed to pick like a bird, then eat pie in front of Ben, who's just been told he can't have any *Fettkuche* 'til he cleans his plate?"

Laura squirmed uneasily, as she waited to see how Eli would respond. She felt his hand under the table, and her fingers squeezed his in response.

"Don'tcha think maybe you should eat everything else first, then have some pie?" Eli's voice was tight, and the muscle in his jaw quivered.

"I don't see why," she shot back. "I'm watching my weight, and the only way I can keep within my calorie count is to leave some food on my plate."

"You could pass up the pie," Mary Ellen suggested.

And I could leave this place and never come back, Laura fumed. Why was everything she did always under scrutiny? Why did she have to make excuses for her behavior all the time? She consoled herself with the thought that soon this would be *her* home, and Eli's parents would only be guests

Things would go the way *she* wanted when that time came.

Laura pushed away from the table. "I'm not really hungry enough for pie anyway. I think I'll go outside for a walk." She threw Eli a scathing look and stomped out of the room. What in the world had she done by marrying a foreigner?

❧

Spring came to the valley early, and with it, the reality that Eli had no plans to leave the Amish faith. Although Laura hadn't come right out and asked, she knew from some of his comments that he was content to remain Plain. Laura would either have to accept her plight in life or leave. Every time she thought about going home to Minnesota without Eli, she felt sick. She would stick it out a bit longer, in the hopes she could eventually get through to him.

The building of the addition began as soon as the snow melted. It couldn't be finished soon enough, as far as Laura was concerned. Mary Ellen Yoder was a pain! In fact, since today was Saturday, and the men were all working on the addition, Eli's mom had suggested she and Laura do some baking.

Martha Rose had taught Laura the basics of baking breads, pies, and cakes, but Mary Ellen seemed to think there was more she should learn. "Today I thought we'd make a brown sugar sponge roll," she said, giving Laura a little nudge toward the cupboard where all the baking supplies were kept.

Laura groaned. "Do we have to? I'm really tired this morning, and I thought it would be nice to sit out on the front porch and watch the men work."

Mary Ellen's forehead wrinkled. "Are ya feelin' poorly?"

Before Laura could respond, her mother-in-law rushed on. 'If ya aren't quite up to snuff, then maybe a good spring tonic 's what you're needin'.'" She opened the cupboard near Laura and plucked out a box of cream of tartar, some sulfur, and a container of Epsom salts. "All we've gotta do is mix some of these in a jar of water. You'll take two or three swallows each mornin' and be feelin' like your old self in no time a'tall."

Laura nearly gagged. She couldn't imagine anything tasting

worse than the mixture Mary Ellen had just suggested. "I'm fine, really. Just didn't sleep well last night. A few cups of coffee and I'll be good to go."

Mary Ellen shrugged and stepped aside. "Suit yourself, but remember the spring tonic, just in case you're still not up to par come mornin'."

Laura nodded and feigned a smile. "Thanks, I'll remember."

ஐ

Preaching was to be held at the Hostetlers' the following day. Laura wasn't looking forward to going, but she saw no way to get out of it. She was tempted to say she was sick, but the thought of Mary Ellen's spring tonic was enough to keep her quiet.

I'll just have to avoid Pauline, Laura told herself as she dressed for church. *Besides, what can that woman say or do to hurt me?*

Several hours later, Laura had her answer. After the service, she and Pauline somehow ended up alone in the kitchen.

"Married life must be agreein' with you," Pauline said in a sarcastic tone.

Laura grabbed a stack of paper plates and headed for the dining room.

"You've put on a few pounds, I see," Pauline called after her.

Laura skidded to a stop and whirled around to face her enemy. "I haven't gained any weight." She raised her chin, so she was looking Pauline right in the eye. "Even if I have, it's none of your concern."

"Eli might not want a plump wife."

Laura held her ground. "I am not plump!"

Pauline shrugged. "Why don't ya quit while you're ahead?"

"What's that supposed to mean?"

"Give Eli his freedom. You'll never make him happy."

Laura was so angry she was visibly shaking, but she couldn't back down now. Pauline Hostetler needed to be put in her place. "I'll have you know, Eli and I are very happy. He tells me how much he loves me every day."

"He probably doesn't want to hurt your fancy feelin's."

Silently, Laura began counting to ten. She couldn't let her temper get the better of her. If someone got wind of it, Eli would be told, then they'd be arguing again. The last thing she needed was for Pauline to hear them quarreling.

"I'm sure you're aware that the Amish don't believe in divorce," Pauline went on. "You're probably countin' on Eli stickin' with you no matter what."

Laura shook her head slowly. "I feel sorry for you, Pauline."

"Well, ya needn't waste your time feelin' sorry for me. You're the one who's headed for trouble." Pauline shook her finger. "When Eli gets fed up and realizes you're not truly one of us, he'll probably ask Bishop Weaver for an annulment. After all, it's not like you're *really* Amish."

Laura set the plates on the table and planted both hands on her hips. "You're wrong about that. Eli will never ask for an annulment, because he loves me. Not you, Pauline. . .me!" Laura stalked out of the room, banging the door as she went.

Laura managed to avoid Pauline the rest of the day, but that was probably because Pauline gave her a wide berth. She served one group of tables, and Laura served another. When it was time for visiting, Pauline excused herself to go to her room, saying she had a headache.

Laura smiled to herself. *Perfect. It couldn't have worked out better if I'd planned it myself.*

❧

As they rode home from church that day, Eli worried. Laura seemed so pensive. Had someone said or done something to upset her? He offered her a smile. "Sure was a *gut* day, wasn't it? So nice we could eat outside again. The only trouble with winter is havin' to cram all our tables into the house or barn where we have worship."

"Uh-huh," Laura mumbled.

"Was ist letz? Is there somethin' troublin' ya?" Eli asked with concern. "You seem kinda down in the dumps."

She shrugged. "Nothing's wrong. Everything's fine. I'm

just getting tired of going to other people's houses and seeing they have indoor plumbing, while our bathroom is yet to be started."

"I said I'd build one just as soon as the addition is done."

"I know, but that might be awhile. Besides, I hate that stupid outhouse!"

Eli squinted his eyes. "Why must ya always find somethin' to complain about? Can't ya just learn to be patient? The Bible says, 'the trying of your faith worketh patience.' It's in the book of James."

"Look," Laura shouted, "I'm a slave to piles of laundry, dirty dishes, and holey socks. My faith in things getting better has definitely been tried, and so has my patience!"

Eli blinked. Was there no pleasing this woman? He'd said he would install indoor plumbing as soon as the addition was finished. That ought to be good enough.

Laura sat on the edge of her seat, pouting. Should she tell Eli about her encounter with Pauline? Sure, she wanted the bathroom done, and she was fed up with working all the time, but that wasn't the real reason she was acting so cross.

Choosing her words carefully, Laura said, "Eli, could I ask you a question?"

He blew out his breath. "Not if it's about indoor plumbin'."

"It's not."

He shrugged. "Okay, ask the question."

She reached across the seat and touched his arm. "Do you think Pauline Hostetler would have made you a better wife?"

Eli lifted one eyebrow and glanced over at Laura. "Pauline? What's she got to do with anything?"

"I just want to know if you think—"

"I can't believe you'd ask me that, Laura. You should know I love ya."

Her eyes filled with unexpected tears. "I thought I did. . until today."

"What happened?"

"Pauline and I had a little discussion." Laura wiped the

tears from her face. "Actually, it was more like an argument."

A look of bewilderment spread across Eli's face. "What were you arguin' about?"

"You."

"Me? Why would you be discussin' me with Pauline?"

"She's the one who brought the subject up," Laura was quick to say. "She thinks I'm no good for you."

"That's ridiculous!"

Laura swallowed hard. "We do argue quite a bit, Eli."

He nodded soberly. *"Jah,* it's true, but Pauline don't know that."

"She's still in love with you."

He groaned. "I've never said or done anything to make Pauline believe I loved her. Not even when she and I were courtin'."

"Well, be that as it may, she's definitely in love with you." Laura sniffed deeply. "She thinks you should see the bishop about an annulment."

Eli pulled sharply on the reins and steered the buggy to the side of the road. "This is more serious than I realized."

Laura's eyes filled with fresh tears. "You—you want to end our marriage?"

He grabbed her around the waist and pulled her close. "Of course not! While we might not see eye-to-eye on everything, you're my wife, and I love you. I plan on us on stayin' married 'til death parts us."

"You don't know how happy I am to hear you say that," Laura said, snuggling against his jacket. "That doesn't take care of things with Pauline, though."

Eli touched her chin lightly with his thumb. "Leave that up to me."

fifteen

"I'm not feeling well. I think I'll stay home from church today," Laura mumbled when Eli tried to coax her out of bed.

"You were feelin' all right last night."

"That was then. This is now."

"If you're worried about Pauline, I've spoken with her *daed,* and he's had a talk with her."

Laura shook her head. "It's not that. Pauline hasn't said a word to me since our last confrontation."

"That's *gut,*" Eli murmured against her ear. "Now get up and go help Mom with breakfast."

"I don't feel like helping today," she said with a deep moan.

Eli touched her forehead. "You ain't runnin' a fever."

"I'm not sick. . .just tired."

"Laura, get up!" Eli said sternly. "You're actin' like a lazy *alte Kuh.*"

Laura bolted upright. "I am not a lazy old cow! I work plenty hard around here. Harder than anyone should be expected to work."

Eli pulled back the covers, hopped out of bed, and stepped into his trousers. He walked across the room to where the water pitcher and bowl sat on top of the dresser. After splashing a handful of water on his face and drying it with a towel, he grabbed his shirt off the wall peg and started for the door. "See ya downstairs in five minutes."

"How dare you order me around!" Laura shouted at the door as it clicked shut. "Maybe I should go home to my parents for awhile. I wonder how you'd like that, Eli Yoder!"

❧

Laura was quiet on the buggy ride to preaching, and during the service, she didn't even sing.

Bishop Weaver gave the last of the three sermons, using Mark 11:25 and 26 as his text. "Jesus' own words said, 'And when ye stand praying, forgive, if ye have ought against any: that your Father also which is in heaven may forgive you your trespasses.' "

How can I forgive Eli when he didn't even say he was sorry? Laura fumed. *That verse doesn't make sense to me.*

Laura was still pouting on the trip home. Eli kept looking at her, and finally he broke the eerie silence between them. "I thought Bishop Weaver's sermon was *gut,* didn't you?"

Laura merely shrugged in response.

"If we don't forgive others, we can't expect God to forgive us."

Laura held her breath, hoping this conversation was leading to an apology. Eli certainly owed her one after this morning.

"I'm not angry anymore, Laura. I forgive ya for bein' so cross this mornin', too."

"Me? It was you shouting orders and not understanding how tired I was," she reminded.

Eli nodded slowly. *"Jah,* I was unkind, and for that I'm sorry. Will ya forgive me?"

A sob caught in her throat, and she slid closer to Eli. "I forgive you," she whispered.

Holding the reins with one hand, Eli took Laura's hand with the other. "Is that all you've got to say?"

She sat there several seconds, then a light dawned. "Oh, yeah. I'm sorry, too."

He grinned and gave her hand a gentle squeeze. "You're forgiven."

Laura leaned her head on his shoulder and sighed. Everything would be all right now.

❧

Johnny and Mary Ellen's new home was finally ready. Since Lewis and Jonas would probably be out of the nest in a few years, it wasn't necessary for the addition to be nearly as large as the main house, so it only had three small bedrooms, a compact bath, roomy kitchen, and an adequate-sized living room. Laura envied Mary Ellen for her indoor plumbing, but it never occurred to her that Eli's mother had waited a long time for such a luxury.

Mary Ellen had been kind enough to leave Eli and Laura some furniture, and Laura was glad to finally have the house all to herself. It would be a welcome relief not to have Eli's mom analyzing everything she said and did. As far as Laura was concerned, the completion of the addition was the best thing to happen since she moved onto the Yoders' farm.

On her first morning as the new mistress of the house, Laura got up late. When she entered the kitchen, she realized Eli was already outside doing his chores. She hurried to start breakfast and was just setting the table when he came inside.

"Your cereal is almost ready," she said with a smile.

He nodded. "Is my lunch packed? I have to leave for work in five minutes."

"Oh, I forgot. I'm running late this morning. Usually your mom gets breakfast while I make your lunch."

"It's okay. I'll just take a few pieces of fruit and some cookies." Eli opened his metal lunch pail and placed two apples, an orange, a handful of peanut butter cookies, and a thermos of milk inside. He took a seat at the table, bowed his head for silent prayer, and dug into the hot oatmeal Laura handed him.

"Can you stop by the store and pick up a loaf of bread on your way home tonight?" Laura asked, taking the seat beside him.

Eli gave her a questioning look.

"I won't have time to do any baking today," she explained "I have clothes to wash, and I want to spend most of the day organizing the house and setting out some of our wedding gifts."

Eli gulped down the last of his milk and stood up. "Guess this one time we can eat store-bought bread. I know it's important for you to set things up." He leaned over and kissed her cheek.

"Ouch! You're prickly!"

"Sorry." Eli grabbed his lunch pail and headed for the door. "See ya later."

Laura waved at his retreating form. When he shut the door, she sighed deeply and surveyed her kitchen. "This house is so big. Where should I begin? I wouldn't want Mary Ellen back again, but a maid sure would be nice."

❧

Laura fretted as she stood at the kitchen sink doing the breakfast dishes. Eli had changed since their marriage. He not only looked different, what with his scratchy beard and all, but he was often snippy and demanding. He still hadn't started the indoor bathroom yet, either, and that exasperated her to no end.

"Work, work, work, that's all I ever do," she muttered. "If Eli tended me the way he does his garden, I'd be in full bloom by now! Whatever happened to romance and long buggy rides to the lake?"

A single tear rolled down her cheek, and she wiped it away with a soapy hand. "Life is so unfair. I gave up a lot to become Eli's wife, and now he won't even listen to me."

The only reminder of Laura's past was her cat, Foosie, who lay curled at her feet. She glanced down at the pampered pet and mumbled, "Too bad Mom and Dad can't come for a visit." She sniffed deeply. "No. . .they're too busy. Dad has his law practice, and Mom runs around like a chicken hunting bugs, trying to meet all her social obligations."

The cat purred contentedly, seemingly unaware of her frustrations.

"You've got life made, you know that?" she scolded.

A knock at the back door drew Laura's attention away from Foosie. *Oh, no. I hope that's not Mary Ellen.*

She dried her hands on her apron and dabbed the corners of her eyes with a handkerchief, then went to answer the door.

To her surprise, Martha Rose and little Ben stood on the porch, each holding a basket. Martha Rose's held freshly baked apple muffins, and Ben's basket was full of ginger cookies.

Laura smiled. She was always glad to see her sister-in-law and that adorable little boy. "Come in. Would you like a cup of tea?"

Martha Rose, her stomach now bulging, lowered herself into a chair. "That sounds mighty *gut*. We can have some of the muffins I brought, too."

Ben spotted Foosie, and he darted over to play with her.

"What brings you by so early?" Laura asked, as she pulled out a chair for herself.

"We're on our way to The Country Store, but we wanted to stop and see you first," Martha Rose answered. "We have an invitation for you and Eli."

Laura's interest was piqued. "What kind of invitation?"

"Since tomorrow's Saturday, and the weather's so nice, Amon and I have decided to take Ben to Paradise Lake for a picnic. We were wonderin' if you and Eli would like to come along."

Laura dropped several tea bags into the pot she'd taken from the stove before she sat down. "Would we ever! At least, I would. If Eli can tear himself away from work long enough, I'm sure he'd have a good time, too."

Martha Rose nodded. "We'll meet ya there around one o'clock. That'll give everyone time enough to do all their chores." She waved her hand. "Speaking of chores—you look awfully tired. Are ya workin' too hard?"

Laura pushed a stray hair back under her head covering and sighed. "I have been feeling a little drained lately. I'll be fine once I get this house organized."

Martha Rose opened her mouth to say something, but Laura cut her off. "What should I bring to the picnic?"

"I thought I'd fix fried chicken, two different salads, and maybe some pickled beet eggs. Why don't ya bring dessert and some kind of beverage?"

"That sounds fine," Laura answered, feeling suddenl

lighthearted. They were going on a picnic, and she could hardly wait!

ಶ

The lake was beautiful, and Laura drank in the peacefulness until she felt her heart would burst.

Martha Rose was busy setting out her picnic foods, and the men were playing ball with little Ben. Laura brought out the brownies and iced mint tea she'd made, and soon the plywood table they brought from home was brimming with delectable food.

Everyone gathered for silent prayer, then the men began to heap their plates full. Laura was the last to dish up, but she only took small helpings of everything. When she came to the tray of pickled beet eggs, a surge of nausea rolled through her stomach like angry ocean waves. Pickled eggs were sickening—little purple land mines, waiting to destroy her insides.

Laura dropped her plate of food and dashed for the woods. Eli ran after her, but he waited until she'd emptied her stomach before saying anything.

"You okay?" he asked with obvious concern.

Laura stood up on wobbly legs. "I'm fine. It was the sight of those pickled eggs. They're disgusting! How can anyone eat those awful things?"

Eli slipped his arm around her waist. "Maybe you've got the flu."

She shook her head. "It was just the eggs. Let's go back to the picnic. I'm fine now, honest."

The rest of the day went well enough, and Laura felt a bit better after drinking some tea. She even joined a friendly game of tag, but she did notice the looks of concern Eli and his sister exchanged. Nobody said anything about her getting sick, and she was glad.

ಶ

A few days later, Laura was outside gathering eggs from the henhouse when she had another attack of nausea. She hadn't eaten any breakfast, so she figured that was the reason.

Besides, the acrid odor of chicken manure was enough to make anyone sick!

Mary Ellen was outside, hanging laundry. She waved to Laura when she started toward the house with her basket of eggs. Laura waved back and hurried on. She was in no mood for a confrontation with her mother-in-law this morning, and she certainly didn't want to get sick in front of her.

"I'm almost finished here," Mary Ellen called. "Come have a cup of coffee."

Laura's stomach lurched at the mere mention of coffee, and she wondered how she could graciously get out of the invitation.

Mary Ellen called to her again. "I know you're busy, but surely you can take a few minutes for a little chat."

"I'll set these eggs inside, then be right over," Laura agreed in defeat. *May as well give in, or Mary Ellen will report to Eli that his wife is unsociable.*

Laura entered the house and deposited the brown eggs in the icebox. Then she went to the sink and pumped enough water for a cool drink. She drank the water slowly and took several deep breaths, which seemed to help some.

"Here goes nothing," she said, opening the back door.

She found Mary Ellen seated at her kitchen table. There were two cups sitting there, and the strong aroma of coffee permeated the air.

Laura's stomach did a little flip-flop as she took a seat. "Uh, would you mind if I had mint tea instead of coffee?"

Mary Ellen stood up. "If that's what you prefer." She went to the cupboard and retrieved a box of tea bags, then poured boiling water from the teapot on the stove into a clean mug.

"You're lookin' kinda peaked this mornin'," Mary Ellen said as she handed Laura the tea.

"I think I might have a touch of the flu."

"You could be in a family way. Have ya thought about that?"

Laura shook her head. "It's the flu. Nothing to worry about."

Mary Ellen eyed her suspiciously. "Would ya like some

shoofly pie or a buttermilk biscuit?"

"I might try a biscuit."

Mary Ellen handed her a basket of warm biscuits. "So, tell me. . .how long's this flu thing been goin' on?"

"Just a few days."

"If it continues, you'd better see Doc Wilson."

Laura grimaced. *There she goes again. . .telling me what to do.* She plucked a biscuit from the basket and spread it lightly with butter. *"Jah,* I'll see the doctor if I don't feel better soon."

٭

Laura's nausea and fatigue continued all that week, but she did her best to hide it from Eli. She didn't want him pressuring her to see the doctor, or worse yet, asking a bunch of questions, the way his mother had.

One morning, Laura decided to go into town for some supplies. She asked Eli to hitch the horse to the buggy before he left for work. As soon as her morning chores were done, she donned her dark bonnet and climbed into the waiting buggy.

When Laura arrived in town, her first stop was the pharmacy. She scanned the shelves until she found exactly what she was looking for. She brought the item to the checkout counter and waited for the clerk to ring it up. He gave her a strange look as he placed the small box inside a paper sack. Laura wondered if she was the first Amish woman who'd ever purchased a home pregnancy kit.

The test couldn't be taken until early the next morning, so when she got home later in the day, Laura found a safe place to hide the kit. The last thing she needed was for Eli to discover it and jump to the wrong conclusions. He would surely think she was pregnant, and she was equally sure she wasn't. She couldn't be. She'd been so careful. Of course, her monthly time was late, but that wasn't too uncommon for her.

Laura waited until Eli left for work the following morning before going to her sewing basket and retrieving the test kit. She slipped it into her apron pocket and rushed to the outhouse.

Moments later, Laura's hands trembled as she held the strip up for examination. It was bright pink. The blood drained from her face, and she steadied herself against the unyielding wall. "Oh, no!" she cried. "It can't be!"

She studied it longer, just to be sure she hadn't read it wrong. It was still pink. "I can't be pregnant. I *won't* be pregnant!"

When she hurried back to the house, Laura's eyes were sore and swollen from crying. She went straight to the kitchen sink and splashed cold water on her face.

I need time to think. No one must know about this—especially not Eli. It will have to remain my secret.

"How long can I keep a secret like this?" she moaned. After some quick calculations, she figured she must be about eight weeks along. In another four to six weeks, she might be starting to show. Besides, if she kept getting sick every day, Eli would either suspect she was pregnant, or decide she was definitely sick and send her to the doctor.

"Oh, Foosie, what am I going to do?" she wailed, looking down at the cat, asleep at her feet. "If I only knew Darla's new phone number, I'd drive back to town and call her."

Laura snapped her fingers. "I do have her address, so I can write a letter."

She moved over to the desk and took out a piece of paper and a pen. She could keep the secret a little longer. Just until Darla responded to her letter.

❧

A whole week went by before Laura heard anything from Darla. Her reply was sympathetic, and she'd devised a plan. Darla would take next Friday off, and Laura was to meet her in Lancaster, in front of a restaurant they both knew well. She would leave the buggy parked there, and Darla would drive her to Philadelphia. She'd already scheduled an appointment for Laura at one of the abortion clinics there.

The following week, Laura pulled her horse and buggy into the restaurant parking lot. Darla was waiting in her sports car. "You've sure gotten yourself into a fine fix," she scolded as

Laura climbed into the passenger's seat. "I knew marrying that Amish guy would bring you nothing but trouble."

"I don't need any lectures," Laura snapped.

Darla reached for a paper sack, lying on the floor by Laura's feet. "Here, you'd better put these on, and let your hair down."

Laura peeked into the bag and frowned. Inside were a navy blue blazer, a few pieces of jewelry, an indigo-colored belt, and a pair of navy pumps. "What are these for?"

"Don't you think it might look a little odd for an Amish woman to go to an abortion clinic? You could even become tomorrow's newspaper headlines," Darla said, shaking her head.

"I hadn't thought about that." Laura untied the strings from her head covering, then pulled the pins out of her bun. Her long hair fell loosely past her shoulders, and she ran her fingers through the ends. Next, she removed the black apron and shoes. She slipped the jacket over her blue, cotton dress, secured the belt around her waist, and stepped into the pumps. The finishing touch was a string of pearls and a matching bracelet.

How ironic, Laura mused. *I've longed for these fancy things, yet right now, I feel strangely guilty about wearing them.*

As though she could read her thoughts, Darla touched Laura's hand. "You're doing the right thing."

Laura nodded soberly. "I suppose."

"That didn't sound too convincing," Darla chided. "Your letter said you didn't want this baby."

"I don't. It's just that—"

"You'll feel better once this is all behind you."

Laura shrugged. "I don't see how I could feel much worse."

sixteen

Laura lifted the teakettle from the back of the stove and poured herself a cup of raspberry tea. This morning she felt better than she had in days. Maybe it was because of the decision she'd made the week before.

She took a seat at the table and let her mind drift back to the drive she and Darla had made to Philadelphia. . . .

Darla had been parking the car at the abortion clinic when a young man carrying a small child walked past. He looked so happy, and the toddler was smiling, too. It caused Laura to think about Eli, and how much he wanted children. He would be a good father, and maybe even a better husband if she gave him what he wanted.

She thought about little Ben—always playful and curious, so full of love, all cute and cuddly. Laura had never cared much for children until she met Ben. She loved that little boy and was sure he loved her in return.

If she were to abort this baby and Eli ever found out, it would be the end of their marriage. Pauline would get her wish, because Eli would probably have their marriage annulled. She'd be banned from the Amish church.

Laura could still see the look on her friend's face when she'd told her she wasn't going to have an abortion. Darla had argued, of course. She'd even tried to make Laura feel guilty for wasting her time. Laura had held firm, realizing that she would do anything to keep Eli—even give birth to his child.

The screen door creaked open, pulling Laura out of her musings. Eli hung his straw hat on a wall peg and went to wash up at the sink. "I hope breakfast's about ready, 'cause I'm hungry as a mule!"

"Pancakes are warming in the oven," Laura said, offering him a smile. "I was wondering if we could talk before we eat, though."

He shrugged. "Sure, what's up?"

She motioned him to sit down, then poured him a cup of tea. "How do you really feel about children, Eli?" she asked, keeping her eyes focused on the cup.

"I've told ya before, someday I hope to fill our house with *kinder.*"

She looked up at him. "Would November be soon enough to start?"

His forehead wrinkled.

"I'm pregnant, Eli. You're gonna be a father in about seven months."

Eli stared at her, disbelief etched on his face. "A *buppli?*"

She nodded.

He jumped up, circled the table, pulled Laura to her feet, and kissed her soundly. "The Lord has answered my prayers!" He pulled away and started for the back door.

"Where are you going?" she called after him.

"Next door. I've gotta share this *gut* news with Mom and Pop!"

❧

Laura hung the last bath towel on the line and wiped her damp forehead with her apron. It was a hot, humid June morning, and she was four months pregnant. She placed one hand on her slightly swollen belly and smiled. A tiny flutter caused her to tremble. "There really is a *buppli* in there," she murmured. So much for calorie counting and weight watching.

She bent down to pick up her empty basket, but an approaching buggy caught her attention. It was coming up the driveway at an unusually fast speed. When it stopped in front of the house, Amon jumped out, his face all red, and his eyes huge as saucers. "Where's Mary Ellen?" he asked Laura.

She pointed toward the addition. "Is something wrong?"

"It's Martha Rose. Her labor's begun, and she refuses to

go to the hospital. She wants her *mamm* to deliver this baby, just like she did Ben."

Laura followed as Amon ran toward the addition. They found Mary Ellen in the kitchen, kneading bread dough. She looked up and smiled. "Ah, so the smell of bread in the makin' drew the two of you inside."

Amon shook his head. "Martha Rose's time has come, and she sent me to get you."

Mary Ellen calmly set the dough aside and wiped her hands on a towel. "Laura, would ya please finish this bread?"

"I thought I'd go along. Martha Rose is my friend, and—"

"There's no point wastin' good bread dough," Mary Ellen said, as though the matter was settled.

Amon was standing by the back door, shifting his weight from one foot to the other. Laura could see he was anxious to get home. "Oh, all right," she finally agreed. "I'll do the bread, but I'm comin' over as soon as it's out of the oven."

It was several hours later when Laura arrived at the Zook farm. She found Amon pacing back and forth in the kitchen. Ben was at the table, coloring a picture. *"Buppli,"* he said, grinning up at her.

Laura nodded. *"Jah,* soon it will come." She glanced over at Amon. "It's not born yet, is it?"

He shook his head. "Don't know what's takin' so long. She was real fast with Ben."

"How come you're not up there with her?" Laura asked.

Amon shrugged. "Mary Ellen said it would be best if I waited down here with the boy."

"Want me to go check?"

"I'd be obliged."

Laura hurried up the stairs. The door to Martha Rose and Amon's room was open a crack, so she walked right in.

Mary Ellen looked up from her position at the foot of the bed. "It's gettin' close. I can see the head now. Push, Martha Rose. . .push!"

Laura's heart began to pound, and her legs felt like two sticks of rubber. She leaned against the dresser to steady herself.

A few minutes later, the lusty cry of a newborn babe filled the room. Laura felt tears stinging her eyes. This was the miracle of birth. She never imagined it could be so beautiful.

"Daughter, you've got yourself a mighty fine girl," Mary Ellen remarked. "Let me clean her up a bit, then I'll hand her right over."

Martha Rose was crying, but Laura knew they were tears of joy. She slipped quietly from the room, leaving mother, daughter, and grandmother alone to share the moment of pleasure.

ぉ

Laura had seen Doc Wilson several times, and other than a bit of anemia, she was pronounced to be in good condition. The doctor prescribed iron tablets to take with her prenatal vitamins, but she still tired easily.

"I'm gonna ask Mom to come over and help out today," Eli said as he prepared to leave for work one morning.

Laura shuffled across the kitchen floor toward him. "Please don't. Your mom's got her hands full helping Martha Rose with the new baby. She doesn't need one more thing to worry about."

Eli shrugged. "Suit yourself, but if you need anything, don't think twice 'bout callin' on her, ya hear?"

She nodded and lifted her face for his good-bye kiss. "Have a *gut* day."

Eli left the house and headed straight for his folks' addition. Laura might think she didn't need Mom's help, but he could see how tired she was. Dark circles under her eyes and swollen feet at the end of the day were telltale signs she needed more rest.

He found Mom in the kitchen, doing the breakfast dishes. "Shouldn't you be headin' for work?" she asked.

He nodded. *"Jah,* but I wanted to talk with you first."

"Anything wrong?" she asked with a look of concern.

He shrugged and ran his fingers through the back of his

hair. "Laura's been workin' too hard, and I think she could use some help."

"Want me to see to it, or are ya thinkin' of hirin' a *maut?*"

"I'd rather it be you, instead of a maid, if ya can find time."

She smiled. "I think I can manage."

"Thanks." Eli grasped the doorknob, but he pivoted back around. "Do ya think Laura's happy, Mom?"

She lifted an eyebrow in question. "Why wouldn't she be? She's married to you, ain't it so?"

He chuckled. *"Jah,* but I ain't no prize." His tone became serious then. "Do ya think she's really content bein' Amish?"

Mom dried her hands on a towel and moved toward him. "Laura chose to become Amish. You didn't force her, neither."

"I know, but sometimes she looks so sad."

"Ah, it's just bein' in a family way. All women get kind of melancholy durin' that time." She patted his arm. "She'll be fine once the *buppli* comes."

Eli gave her a hug. "You're probably right. I'm most likely worryin' over nothin'."

&

Laura wasn't due until the end of the November, but five days before her and Eli's first anniversary, she went into labor. When Eli arrived home from work that afternoon, he found her lying on the couch, holding her stomach and writhing in pain.

"What is it, Laura?" he asked, rushing to her side.

"I think the baby's coming."

"When did the pains start?"

"Around noon."

Eli grasped her hand. "What does Mom have to say?"

Laura squeezed his fingers. "She doesn't know."

"What?" Eli could hardly believe Laura hadn't called on Mom. She'd delivered many babies, so she was bound to know if it was time.

"I wasn't sure if it even was labor at first," Laura explained. "But then my water broke, and—"

Eli jumped up and dashed across the room.

"Where are you going?" she called.

"To get Mom!"

⬝⬝

Laura leaned her head against the sofa pillow and stiffened when another contraction came. "Oh, God, please help me!" It was the first real prayer Laura had ever uttered, and now she wasn't sure God was even listening. Why would He care about her, when she'd never really cared about Him? She'd only been pretending to be a Christian. Was this her punishment for lying to Eli and his family?

Moments later, Eli came bounding into the room, followed by his mother.

"How far apart are the pains?" Mary Ellen asked as she approached the couch.

"I–I don't know for sure. About two or three minutes, I think," Laura answered tearfully. "Oh, it hurts so much! I think Eli should take me to the hospital."

Mary Ellen did a quick examination, and when she was done, she announced, "You waited too long. The *buppli* is comin' now."

Eli started for the kitchen. "I'll get some towels and warm water."

"Don't leave me, Eli!"

"Calm down," Mary Ellen chided. "He'll be right back. In the meantime, I want you to do exactly as I say."

Laura's first reaction was to fight the pain, but Mary Ellen was a good coach, and soon Laura began to cooperate. Eli stood nearby, holding her hand and offering soothing words.

"One final push and the *buppli* should be here," Mary Ellen said.

Laura did as she was instructed, and moments later the babe's first cry filled the room.

"It's a boy! You have a son, Eli," Mary Ellen announced.

Laura lifted her head from the pillow. "Let me see him. I want to make sure he has ten fingers and ten toes."

"In a minute. Let Eli clean him a bit," Mary Ellen instructed.

"I need to finish up with you."

"Mom, could ya come over here?" Eli called from across the room. His voice sounded strained, and Laura felt a wave of fear wash over her.

"What is it? Is something wrong with our son?"

"Just a minute, Laura. I want Mom to take a look at him first."

Laura rolled onto her side, trying to see what was happening. Eli and Mary Ellen were bent over the small bundle wrapped in a towel, lying on top of an end table. She heard whispering but couldn't make out their words.

"What's going on?" she called. "Tell me now, or I'm going to come see for myself."

Eli rushed to her side. "Stay put. You might start bleedin' real heavy if ya get up too soon."

Laura drew in a deep breath and grabbed hold of Eli's shirt-sleeve. "What's wrong?"

"The child's breathin' seems a bit irregular," Mary Ellen said. "I think we should take him to the hospital."

"*Jah,*" Eli agreed. "It might not be a bad idea for Laura to be seen, too."

ॐ

Laura had only gotten a glimpse of her son before they rushed him into the hospital nursery, but what she did see concerned her greatly. The baby *wasn't* breathing right. He looked kind of funny, too. He had a good crop of auburn hair, just like Laura's, but there was something else. . .something she couldn't put her finger on.

"Relax and try to rest," Eli said as he took a seat in the chair next to Laura's hospital bed. "The doctor's lookin' at little David right now, and—"

"David?" Laura repeated. "You named our son without asking me?"

Eli's face flamed. "I—uh—thought we'd talked about namin' the baby David, if it was a boy."

She nodded slowly. "I guess we did. I just thought—"

Laura's sentence was interrupted when Dr. Wilson and another man entered the room. His expression told her all she needed to know. There *was* something wrong with the baby.

"This is Dr. Hayes," Dr. Wilson said. "He's a pediatrician and has just finished examining your son."

"Tell us. . .is there somethin' wrong with David?" Eli asked, jumping to his feet.

Dr. Hayes put a hand on Eli's shoulder. "Sit down, Son."

Eli complied, but Laura could see the strain on his face. She felt equally discomforted.

"We still need to run a few more tests," the doctor said, "but we're fairly sure your boy has Down's syndrome."

"Are ya sayin' he's retarded?" Eli asked.

"Quite possibly, only we prefer to call it 'handicapped' or 'disabled.' The baby has an accumulation of fluid on his lungs. It's fairly common with Down's. We can clear it out, but he will no doubt be prone to bronchial infections—especially while he's young."

Laura was too stunned to say anything at first. This had to be a dream—a terrible nightmare. This couldn't be happening to her.

"Once we get the lungs clear, you should be able to take the baby home," Dr. Hayes continued.

"Take him home?" Laura pulled herself to a sitting position. "Did you say, 'take him home'?"

The doctor nodded, and Eli reached for her hand. "Laura, we can get through this. We—"

Laura jerked her hand away. "Are you kidding? We've just been told our son has Down's syndrome, and you're saying 'we can get through this'?" She shook her head slowly. "The baby isn't normal, Eli. He doesn't belong with us."

Eli studied Laura a few seconds. "Who does he belong with?"

"If he's handicapped, he belongs in a home."

seventeen

The baby was brought to Laura the following day, and she could barely look at him. The nurse held David up and showed her he had ten fingers and ten toes.

Fingers that are short and stubby, Laura thought bitterly. She noticed the child's forehead. It sloped slightly, and his skull looked broad and short. The distinguishing marks of Down's syndrome were definitely there. The doctor had explained that David might also be likely to have heart problems, hearing loss, or poor vision. He said Down's syndrome was a genetic disorder, resulting from extra chromosomes.

How could this have happened? Laura screamed inwardly. She looked away and told the nurse to take the baby back to the nursery. Swiping at her tears, she reached for the telephone next to her bed. It was time to call Mom and Dad. They needed to know the baby had been born.

"How am I going to tell them their first grandchild is handicapped?" she moaned.

Mom answered the phone, and she was understandably shocked when Laura gave her the news. Laura had hoped she might offer to come to Pennsylvania, but after Mom said how sorry she was, she made some excuse about her hectic schedule, said the baby should be put in a home for special children, and hung up the phone. Dad hadn't been at home, so she had no idea how he would have reacted.

Laura was crying when Eli entered the room carrying a potted plant. "I got ya an African violet from the Beachys' greenhouse, and—" He dropped it to the nightstand and moved quickly to the bed. *"Was ist letz?* Is it something about David?"

She hiccupped loudly and pulled herself to a sitting position. When she felt she could speak without crying, Laura plunged ahead. "I just got off the phone with my mother."

"What did she say?"

"She said she was sorry to hear our sad news and that David should be put in a home."

Eli sank to the edge of her bed and reached for her hand.

"She's right, Eli. A disabled child takes a lot of work."

Eli frowned deeply. "David has just as much right to live a normal life as any other child."

"But he's not normal," Laura argued.

"Mom will be there to help whenever you need her."

The full meaning of Eli's words slammed into her chest. Laura shook her head, and another set of tears streamed down her cheeks. "I can't do this, Eli. Please don't ask it of me."

Eli rubbed his thumb gently back and forth across her knuckles. "God gave us David. He must have a reason for choosin' us as his parents, so we'll love him. . .cherish him. . . protect him."

Laura's eyes widened. "God was cruel to allow such a thing!"

"God knows what's best for each of us. The book of Romans tells us that all things work together for good to them that love God," Eli said softly. He pointed to the African violet. "Just like this plant needs to be nourished, so does our son. God will give us the strength and love we need to raise him."

She looked away. It was obvious Eli planned to have the last word. Apparently, her thoughts and feelings didn't matter one bit. For the first time since she'd laid eyes on Eli Yoder, Laura wished they had never met.

❧

Laura went home from the hospital the following morning, but the baby would have to stay a few more days. The doctors thought he might be ready to take home next week, so this gave Laura a short reprieve. She needed some time to decide what to do about the problem.

Eli had taken a few hours off work in order to pick her up at the hospital, but he'd already gone back to his job in

Lancaster. Laura was alone and hoped to find some answers before he returned home.

She poured herself a cup of chamomile tea and curled up on the living room couch. Reliving her dialog with Eli at the hospital, Laura's heart sank to the pit of her stomach. Eli thought they should keep David.

She closed her eyes and tried to shut out the voice in her head. *God is punishing me for pretending to be religious. I tricked Eli into marrying me by making him think I'd accepted his beliefs.*

Laura's eyes snapped open when she heard a distant clap of thunder. She stared out the window. Dark clouds hung in the sky, like a shroud encircling the entire house.

"The sky looks like I feel," she moaned. "My life is such a mess. I should have listened to Darla and gone into that abortion clinic."

The realization of what she'd said hit Laura with such intensity, she thought she'd been struck with a lightning bolt. "Oh, no! Dear, Lord, no!" she sobbed. "You're punishing me for wanting an abortion, not just for lying to Eli about my religious convictions." She clenched her fists into tight little balls. "That's why David was born with Down's syndrome!"

Laura fell back on the sofa pillows and cried until there were no more tears. Nearly an hour later, she sat up again, dried her eyes, and stood up. She knew what she had to do. She scrawled a quick note to Eli, placed it on the kitchen table, and went upstairs.

&

"Laura, I'm home!" Eli set his lunch pail on the cupboard. No sign of Laura in the kitchen. He moved through the rest of the downstairs, calling her name. She wasn't in any of the rooms.

She must be upstairs restin'. She's been through a lot this week. I'd better let her sleep awhile.

Eli went back to the kitchen. He'd fix himself a little snack, then go outside and get started on the evening chores.

There was an apple-crumb pie in the refrigerator, which

Mom had brought over last night. He grabbed a piece, along with a jug of milk, and placed them on the table. Not until he took a seat, did Eli see the note lying on the table. He picked it up and read it.

Dear Eli,

It pains me to write this letter, even more than the physical pain I endured in childbirth. I know you don't understand, but I can't take care of David, so I'm going home to my parents.

I have a confession to make. I'm not who you think I am—I'm not really a believer. I only pretended to be one so you would marry me. The truth is, I had hoped that once we were married you might decide to leave the Amish faith and become part of my world. I tried to be a good wife, but I could never measure up.

Pauline was right when she said she would be better for you. It would have saved us all a lot of heartache if you'd married her instead of me.

Do what you need to about ending our marriage. I know divorce is not acceptable, but maybe once you've explained things to Bishop Weaver, he will agree to an annulment. Our marriage was based on lies from the very beginning, so it was never a true marriage at all.

I'm not deserving of your forgiveness, but please know, I do love you.

Always,
Laura

The words on the paper blurred. Eli couldn't react. Couldn't think. He let the note slip from his fingers, and a deep sense of loss gnawed at his insides. *Laura wouldn't pack up and leave without speaking with me first. . .without trying to work things out.*

He propped his elbows on the table and cradled his head in

his hands, as a well of emotion rose in his chest. "Oh, Laura. . . I didn't know."

&

During her first few days at home, Laura slept late, picked at her food, and tried to get used to all the modern conveniences she'd previously taken for granted. Nothing seemed to satisfy her. She was exhausted, crabby, and more depressed than she'd ever been in her life. Things had changed at home. Maybe it was she who'd changed, for she now felt like a misfit.

Today was her and Eli's first anniversary, and she was miserable. As she sat at the kitchen table toying with the scrambled eggs on her plate, Laura thought about their wedding day. She could still hear Bishop Weaver quoting Scriptures about marriage. She could almost feel the warmth of Eli's hand as they repeated their vows. She'd promised to love, honor, and obey her husband. A painful lump lodged in her throat as she realized that she'd done none of those things. She deserved whatever punishment God handed down.

Mom came into the kitchen, interrupting Laura's thoughts. "This came in the mail," she said, handing Laura a letter. It was postmarked Lancaster, Pennsylvania.

Laura's fingers shook as she tore open the envelope, then began to read.

Dear Laura,

I knew you were upset about the baby, and I'm trying to understand. What I don't get is how you could just up and leave, without even tryin' to talk to me first. Don't ya realize how much David and I need you? Don't ya know how much I love you?

David's breathin' better now, and the doctors let him come home. Mom watches him when I'm at work, but it's you he's needin'. Won't ya please come home?

Love,
Eli

Tears welled up in Laura's eyes and spilled over onto the front of her blouse. Eli didn't seem angry. In fact, he wanted her to come home. He hadn't even mentioned her lies. Had he forgiven her? Did Eli really love her, in spite of all she'd done?

Maybe he doesn't believe me. He might think I made every-thing up, because I couldn't deal with our baby being born handicapped. He might want me back just so I can care for his child.

Laura swallowed hard. No matter how much she loved Eli and wanted to be with him, she knew she couldn't go back. She was a disgrace to the Amish religion, and she had ruined Eli's life.

æ

The days dragged by, and Laura thought she would die of boredom. The weather was dreary and cold, and even though Mom tried to encourage her to get out and socialize, Laura stayed to herself most of the time. She thought modern con-veniences would bring happiness, but they hadn't. Instead of watching TV or playing computer games, she preferred to sit in front of the fire and knit or read a book.

It was strange, but Laura missed the familiar farm smells— fresh-mown hay stacked neatly in the barn, the horses' warm breath on a cold winter day, and even the wiggly, grunting piglets, always squealing for more food. Laura was reminded of something Eli had once said, for much to her surprise, she even missed the predictable wake-up call of the rooster each morning.

By the middle of December, Laura felt stronger physically, but emotionally she was still a mess. Would she ever be able to pick up the pieces of her life and go on without Eli? Could she forgive herself for bringing such misery into their lives?

If God was punishing her, why did Eli have to suffer as well? He was a kind, Christian man who deserved a normal, healthy baby. He'd done nothing to warrant this kind of pain. How could the Amish refer to God as "a God of love and life"?

Laura sat on the living room couch, staring at the Christmas tree, yet not really seeing it. *What's Eli doing right now? No doubt he and the baby will be spending the holiday with his parents.*

She glanced at her parents. They were sitting in their respective recliners, Dad reading the newspaper and Mom working on Christmas cards. They didn't seem to have a care in the world. Didn't they know how much she was hurting? Did they think this was just another typical Christmas?

A sudden knock at the front door drew Laura out of her musings. She looked over at the mantel clock. Who would be coming by at nine o'clock at night, and who would knock rather than use the doorbell?

Dad stood up. "I'll get it."

Laura strained to hear the voices coming from the hall. She couldn't be sure who Dad was talking to, but it sounded like a woman. *Probably one of Mom's lady friends, or someone from Dad's office.* She leaned against the sofa pillows and tried not to eavesdrop.

"Laura, someone is here to see you," Dad said as he entered the living room with a woman.

Laura's mouth dropped open and she leaped from the couch. "Martha Rose! What are you doing here? Is Eli with you?" She stared at the doorway, half expecting, half hoping Eli might step into the room.

Martha Rose shook her head. "I've come alone. Only Amon knows I'm here. I left him plenty of my milk, and he agreed to care for baby Amanda and little Ben so I could make the trip to see you." She smiled. "The bus ride only took a little over twenty-seven hours, and Amon knows I won't be gone long. Besides, if he runs into any kind of problem with the *kinder,* he can always call on Mom."

Laura's heart began to pound as she tried to digest all that Martha Rose had said. "What's wrong? Has someone been hurt? Is it Eli?"

Martha Rose held up her hand. "Eli's fine. . .at least physically." She glanced at Laura's folks, then back at Laura. "Could we talk in private?"

Laura looked at Mom and Dad. They both shrugged and turned to go. "We'll be upstairs if you need us," Mom said.

"Thanks," Laura mumbled. Her brain felt like it was in a fog. Why had Martha Rose traveled all the way from Pennsylvania to Minnesota if there was nothing wrong at home? Home—was that how she thought of the farmhouse she and Eli had shared for the past year? Wasn't this her home—here with Mom and Dad? She studied her surroundings. Everything looked the same, yet it felt so different. It was like trying to fit into a pair of shoes that were too small.

"Laura, are you okay?" Martha Rose asked, placing a hand on Laura's trembling shoulder.

"I—uh—didn't expect to see you tonight." Laura motioned toward the couch. "Please, have a seat. Let me take your shawl. Would you like some tea or hot chocolate?" She was rambling but couldn't seem to help herself.

Martha Rose took off her shawl and draped it over the back of the couch, then she sat down. "Maybe somethin' to drink but after we talk."

Laura sat beside her. "What's so important that you would come all this way by bus?"

"My brother has been so upset since you left. He told me he wrote a letter, askin' you to come home."

"Did he also tell you I've been lying to him all these months?"

"About bein' a believer?"

Laura nodded.

"Jah, he mentioned that, too."

"Then you understand why I can't go back." Laura swallowed hard. "I asked Eli to see the bishop about an annulment, but I've heard nothing from him on the subject."

Martha Rose reached inside her apron pocket and pulled out a small Bible. She opened it and began reading. " 'If any brother hath a wife that believeth not, and she be pleased to dwell with him, let him not put her away.' " She smiled.

"That's found in the book of First Corinthians."

Laura's eyes widened. "Are you saying Eli could choose to stay with me, even though I'm not a believer?"

Martha Rose nodded. "It doesn't have to be that way, though."

"What do you mean?"

"You could give your heart to Jesus right now. He wants you to accept His death as forgiveness for your sins. First John 3:23 says, 'And this is His commandment, that we should believe on the name of His Son Jesus Christ, and love one another, as He gave us commandment.' "

As Martha Rose continued to read from the Bible, Laura fell under deep conviction—she was finally convinced of the truth in God's Word—and soon tears began streaming down her face. "Oh, Martha Rose, you have no idea how much I've sinned. I did a terrible thing, and now God is punishing me. How can I ever believe He would forgive me?"

"Romans 3:23 says, 'For all have sinned, and come short of the glory of God.' If we ask, God will forgive any sin." Martha Rose clasped Laura's hand.

"I—I—didn't even want our baby. When I first found out I was pregnant, I had an English friend drive me to Philadelphia—to an abortion clinic."

The shocked look on her sister-in-law's face told Laura all she needed to know. Eli and his family thought this was a terrible sin, and so must God.

"Why, Laura? Why would ya do such a thing?"

"I was afraid of having a child. I know it's a vain thing to say, but I wanted to keep my trim figure." She gulped. "Even more than that, I wanted Eli all to myself. I couldn't go through with it, though. I loved Eli too much, and I wanted to give him a child." Laura closed her eyes and drew in a shuddering breath. "God's punishment was David. He gave us a disabled child."

"God don't work thataway," Martha Rose insisted. "He loves you, just as He loves the special child He gave you and

Eli. God wants you to ask His forgiveness and surrender your life to Him."

"I want to be forgiven," Laura admitted. "I want to change, but I don't know if I have enough faith to believe."

Martha Rose took hold of Laura's hand. "All ya need to do is take that first little step by acceptin' Jesus as your Savior. Then, through studyin' His Word and prayin', your faith will be strengthened. Would ya like to pray right now and ask Jesus into your heart?"

Laura didn't even hesitate. "Would you help me? I don't really know how to pray."

As Martha Rose and Laura prayed, Laura found the forgiveness she so desperately needed. When she went to bed that night, a strange warmth crept through her body. She felt God's presence for the very first time and knew without reservation that she was a new person, because of His Son, Jesus. Martha Rose was sleeping across the hall in the guest room, and Laura thanked God she had come.

❧

Laura clung tightly to Martha Rose's hand as they stepped down from the bus. She was almost home, and even though she still had some doubts about her ability to care for a handicapped child, it was comforting to know she would have God to help her. She scanned the faces of those waiting to pick up passengers. There was no sign of Eli or Amon.

"Are you sure they knew we were coming?" Laura asked Martha Rose, feeling a sense of panic rise in her throat.

"I sent the telegram, so I'm certain they'll be here," Martha Rose said, leading Laura toward the bus station. "Let's get outta the cold and wait for 'em inside."

The women had no more than taken seats when Amon walked up. He was alone.

Laura felt like someone had punched her in the stomach. "Where's Eli? Didn't he come with you?" *Maybe he's changed his mind about wanting you back. Could be that he's already gotten the marriage annulled,* a troubling voice taunted.

"Eli's at the hospital," Amon said, placing a hand on Laura's shoulder.

Her stomach churned like whipping cream about to become butter. "The hospital? Is it the baby? Is David worse?"

Amon shook his head. "There was an accident today."

"An accident? What happened?" Martha Rose asked, her face registering the concern Laura felt.

"Eli cut his hand at work, on one of them fancy electric saws."

Laura covered her mouth with her hand. "How bad?"

"He lost part of one finger, but the doc said he should still be able to use the hand once everything heals."

"Oh, my dear, sweet, Eli!" Laura cried. "Haven't you already been through enough? If only I hadn't run away. If only—"

Martha Rose held up her hand. "No, Laura. You can't go blamin' yourself. Just as David's birth defect is no one's fault, this was an accident, plain and simple. In time, Eli will heal and be back at work."

Laura looked down at her clasped hands, feeling like a small child learning to walk. "Guess my faith is still pretty weak. I'd better pray about it, huh?"

Martha Rose nodded. *"Jah,* prayer is always the best way."

❧

Eli was lying in his hospital bed, fighting the weight of heavy eyelids. Against his wishes the nurse had given him a shot for pain, and now he was feeling so sleepy he could hardly stay awake. Amon had left for the bus station over an hour ago. What was taking so long? Maybe Laura had changed her mind and stayed in Minneapolis. Maybe. . .

"Eli? Eli?" A gentle voice filled his senses. Was he dreaming or was it just wishful thinking?

He felt the touch of a soft hand against his uninjured hand, and his eyes snapped open. "Laura?"

She nodded, her eyes filled with tears. "Oh, Eli, I'm so sorry!" She rested her head on his chest and sobbed. "Can you ever forgive me for running away. . .for lying about my relationship to God. . .for wanting you to change when it was really me who needed changing?"

Eli stroked the top of her head, noting with joy that she was wearing her covering. "I've already forgiven you, my love, but I must ask your forgiveness, too."

She raised her head and stared into his eyes. "For what? You've done nothing."

He swallowed against the lump in his throat. "For not bein' understanding enough." He touched her chin with his good hand. "I think I expected too much, and sometimes I spoke harshly, instead of tryin' to see things from your point of view. If I'd been a better husband, maybe you would've found Christ's love sooner."

Laura shook her head. "It wasn't your fault. I was stubborn and selfish. That's what kept me from turning to God. I believed I could do everything in my own strength. I thought I could have whatever I wanted, and it didn't matter who I hurt in the process." She sniffed deeply. "When I finally turned away from sin and found forgiveness through Christ, I became a new creature." She leaned closer, so their lips were almost touching. "I love you, Eli Yoder."

He smiled. "And I love you, Laura Yoder. Christmas is only a few days away, and I'm convinced it's gonna be our best Christmas ever." He sealed his promise with a tender kiss.

"Ich wehl dich," Laura whispered.

"I choose you, too," he murmured, then drifted off to sleep.

epilogue

Laura stood at the sink, peeling potatoes for the stew they would have for supper. She gazed out the window at Eli and their two-year-old son as they romped in the snow. David was doing so well, and she praised and thanked God for him every day. He was such an agreeable, loving child. How could she have ever not wanted him? Eli had been right all along. David was special—a wonderful gift from God.

A soft "meow" drew Laura's attention from the window. She turned toward the sound, and her lips formed a smile. Foosie was running across the kitchen floor, and their nine-month-old daughter, Barbara, was in fast pursuit.

Laura chuckled at the sight of her perfect little girl, up on her knees, chasing that poor cat and pulling on its tail. No wonder Foosie preferred to be outdoors these days.

"Life couldn't be any better," Laura whispered. "I've made peace with Pauline Hostetler. My parents live on a small farm nearby. I've learned that Eli's folks really do care about me. I have two *wunderbaar* children and a *gut* husband who loves us all more'n anything, and—" She looked up. "And I have You, Lord. Thank You for takin' a fancy, spoiled English woman and turnin' her into a plain Amish wife, who loves You so much. God, You've truly blessed me!"

A Letter To Our Readers

Dear Reader:

In order that we might better contribute to your reading enjoyment, we would appreciate your taking a few minutes to respond to the following questions. We welcome your comments and read each form and letter we receive. When completed, please return to the following:

Rebecca Germany, Fiction Editor
Heartsong Presents
PO Box 719
Uhrichsville, Ohio 44683

1. Did you enjoy reading *Plain and Fancy* by Wanda E. Brunstetter?

   ❑ Very much! I would like to see more books by this author!

   ❑ Moderately. I would have enjoyed it more if

   _____

   _____

2. Are you a member of **Heartsong Presents**?   Yes ❑ No ❑
   If no, where did you purchase this book?_____

   _____

3. How would you rate, on a scale from 1 (poor) to 5 (superior), the cover design?_____

4. On a scale from 1 (poor) to 10 (superior), please rate the following elements.

   _____ Heroine   _____ Plot

   _____ Hero   _____ Inspirational theme

   _____ Setting   _____ Secondary characters

5. These characters were special because_____

_____

_____

6. How has this book inspired your life?_____

_____

_____

7. What settings would you like to see covered in future
   Heartsong Presents books?_____

_____

_____

8. What are some inspirational themes you would like to see
   treated in future books?_____

_____

_____

9. Would you be interested in reading other **Heartsong
   Presents** titles?   Yes ❏   No ❏

10. Please check your age range:
    ❏ Under 18   ❏ 18-24   ❏ 25-34
    ❏ 35-45   ❏ 46-55   ❏ Over 55

Name _____

Occupation _____

Address _____

City _____ State _____ Zip _____

Email _____